I0643307

Arthur Greaves

Bubbles from the Deep

Sonnets and Other Poems, Dramatic and Personal

Arthur Greaves

Bubbles from the Deep
Sonnets and Other Poems, Dramatic and Personal

ISBN/EAN: 9783337343057

Printed in Europe, USA, Canada, Australia, Japan

Cover: Foto ©Andreas Hilbeck / pixelio.de

More available books at **www.hansebooks.com**

BUBBLES FROM THE DEEP,

Sonnets and other Poems,

DRAMATIC AND PERSONAL,

BY

ARTHUR GREAVES.

PRINTED FOR THE AUTHOR.

1873.

Entered according to Act of Congress in the year 1873 by

W. HOWARTH,

In the office of the Librarian of Congress, at Washington, D. C.

INDEX.

MISCELLANEOUS PEICES.

DEDICATION.

Go forth, my Life, and thy dear kindred seek;
    Mourn with the sad, and with the glad rejoice;
For wondering souls, their sweet emotion speak;
    For voiceless passion, be thou hence a voice.
And would'st thou well thy various task fulfil,
    With various minds, show thou a various mood;
Where thou find rapture, rapture leave thou still;
    In hearts that languish, sweetly stir the blood.
Seek him that loves, and join his frenzied hour;
    Seek him that hates, and blend his hate with love;
Seek him that loves and seeks that heavenly power
    That clothes old objects with new power to move:
All thou hast been in hours thou wast the best,
Be thou to all who claim thee for their guest.

SONNETS.

BRITANNIA TO COLUMBIA.

I.

Thy hand, my younger, though not youngest brother;
    Peace let it be between us hence forever;
Thy cause be mine—be witness for each other;
    Stilled be the heart that would our union sever.
I struck thy youth—well thou returned'st the blow—
    I gave thee right to feel I struck in hate;
I would not say, God speed, when thou would'st go
    To fill the place assigned by matchless fate.
The blow was blind, but came not from the heart;
    Still mine the fault, and mine to be forgiven:
In blood, in tongue, in faith, we have one part;
    He braves God's wrath, by whom such ties are
      riven.
Let that sole strife have power to move our blood,
That victory gives to greatest power for good.

(5)

II.

Thou'st nought of mine; I covet nought of thine;
　　Still may not justice sometimes taint one's honor?
Should I yield ought, though none might say 'twas
　　mine,
　　　Might not my name, then, bear some stain upon
　　　her?
What deeds are done—but none may I accuse—
　　For name and fame, and lust of brute dominion;
How have—how still do men their power abuse,
　　To win base gain, and gain men's base opinion!
But with the time my fate must change her scope,
　　And build right future o'er a wrongful past;
The world's great heart I would inspire with hope
　　Nought sinks that on the stream of right is cast.
Would'st thou, from hence, plight me thy brother's
　　hand,
The world's best hope, our union might command.

SONNETS.

I.

The sun makes bright again that hour in May,
    Wherein these eyes this wondrous world did greet;
And as swift Time repeats my natal day,
    More wondrous grow the wondrous shows I meet.
We've passed by April with her smile and frown,
    And, though in tears, May comes with hopeful
        mien;
The birds and flowers their nuptial trust have shown
    Life will be crowned in gracious summer's reign.
Birds, flowers, and I, are here; we know not why;
    But that we're here, shall we not deem it well?
All gladly live, why not as gladly die?
    Though whither hence, no tongue has leave to tell.
Ah! in that power that raised us from the dust,
In death, as life, we have no power to trust.

II.

Relentless Time has stolen another year;
    And still, I own, he proves a gentle thief;
He steals my years, still bringing death more near;
    But for his wrongs, I steal from him relief.
What passions in my younger moments grew,
    Such as oft leave but ashes in their place,
Bear still the strength and glow they ever knew,
    Or else from Time they steal a softer grace.
With years, Time steals no feeling from my heart,
    Nor with new limits bounds my ranging mind;
He steals the forms that glowing thoughts impart,
    But with new life, he leaves their soul behind.
Let Time then steal, while life may thus remain;
While heart and brain their vigor thus retain.

III.

My spring has passed; I've met my summer sun,
    Yet little fruit or bloom my life has shown;
My noon has come; my work has scarce begun;
    The work to do, the morn has scarce made known.
But shall my soul still sleep in fruitless rest,
    And with my spring, all fruitful life decay?
Or shall my summer, autumn life invest
    With fruit, to grace some early winter day?

The snowdrop blooms while snow is on the ground;
   The daisy smiles ere yet the fields are green;
The rose is later in his glory found,
   And still his fruit is ere the winter seen:
Thus some bloom late, yet fruit before they fall;
Shall I do so, or bear no fruit at all?

IV.

This vague, unresting sentiment I feel—
   As when dim boding o'er my heart portends—
Seems to my soul its destiny's appeal
   That life serve not, alone, this body's ends.
Eating, drinking—new, ill fangled, modes of dress—
   Making of house and equipage a show—
The wealth and power, life wasted to possess,
   Feed not, alone, all life the soul would know.
The brute can eat what does his want suffice;
   His mode of dress is nature's wise concern;
To place supreme, like man, he seeks to rise—
   All instinct claims, he wisely can discern:
Still, nature bounds his needs by brutely aims;
But on this life my soul has human claims.

V.

Some envious power, steering my wandering bark,
    Still turns its drift against my wish and will—
Aims winged with hope, turns from their glimmer-
      ing mark,
    Changing their course, some unseen end to fill.
Ever hungering fancy sees some distant joy—
    In trustful mood, sees how its prize to gain;
Then heart and brain their willing strength employ;
    But ever distant does the joy remain.
Still may the dreams that spelled my youthful mind,
    That took all hues that magic fancy gave,
In later years, perhaps, some fulfilment find,
    Though never such as fancy wished to have:
My dreams of youth might future life presage,
Though youthful dreams be not fulfilled with age.

VI.

List! Music's voice, compound of heavenly chords,
    Breathes through this stillness from the distant
      dale;
Its melting tones we hear, but still no words:
    Nor words it needs, to tell its tender tale.
The heart can speak with mute, unworded voice,
    And float its burden on the lifeless air;

In joy can bid the distant heart rejoice,
 And claim its sympathy in grief and care.
Of music, love must ever be the soul,
 Still varying with love's ever varying form ;
It can the heart's most various moods control
 By tones that bear a universal charm :
All kindred love, concealed in kindred hearts,
Takes life and form, from fire its voice imparts.

VII.

Ah, let me hear again that melody !
 While music pleases, that must still be dear !
It brings me back the precious memory
 Of that sweet hour when first it thrilled my ear.
'Twas night, and still—all but the dreaming trees,
 Which seemed to tremble with my own delight;
Or, perhaps, the bird that charms the sleeping breeze
 When summer moons flood earth with shimmering
  light.
The world, that rapturous hour, was all my own,
 Fragrant with incense from the summer bloom,—
My heart in solitude, the past unknown,
 While those dear tones woke in the heavenly
  gloom.
With that rich hour wise memory will not part;
Too few such hours can memory give the heart.

VIII.

Mozart's sweet thought that night my favorite sung,
    And in such tones! how could my heart forget!
Delicious frenzy o'er my soul she flung,
    And rapture's tears within my eyes were set.
She bore an angel's power from bounteous heaven!
    The hushéd throng proclaimed her heav'nly might;
To her the boon and precious right were given,
    To fill their trembling hearts with heaven's delight.
I know not earth when I such music hear;
    My soul flies heavenward on ecstatic wings;
Such moments, brightest gleams of heaven appear;
    From heaven to earth, heaven's purest joy it
        brings.
Heaven favored child! what sacred wealth was
        thine!
Poor me, how rich! when thy dear song was mine!

IX.

So does mere trembling motion of the air
    Set up this sweet commotion in my soul—
Awake a sense no other sense may share,
    But which may still, each other sense control.
When brain is sleeping in its stagnant thought,
    The heart deaf, too, to fancy's upward call,
Thus sweetly are they from their torpor brought,
    If on the ear this thrilling motion fall.

Then earth-bound joys, no longer bound to earth,
    All wildly with sweet heavenward passion glow;
Passion now aiding struggling thought to birth,
    Clothing, anew, old thoughts in beauteous show.
O wondrous is that power of wondrous mind,
That forms such sweetness from mere quivering
    wind.

X.

I breathe the music of the poet's line,
    Then does my soul become poetical;
In his sweet frenzy, being made divine,
    Then on the earth fresh light and beauty fall.
We see the magnet, charged with mystic power,
    Dull metal with a kindred force endue;
So am I in the poet's ruling hour,
    Illumed to see the heavenly good and true.
As suns to satellites, their stuff the same,
    By less and more, changing to dark and light,
Mere magnitude, in suns, creating flame
    That saves the lesser world from frozen night:
So does his soul, our thoughts and passions one,
Give living flame to light and warm my own.

XI.

With him I rise to that empyrean sphere
  Where thoughts, as flowers, are clothed in fadeless
    beauty;
There, in sure tones, my inward senses hear
  Eternal voices teach the soul's best duty.
He calls me up with soft yet sure command
  To realms where does my soul its home descry;
His power compels, and in his charmèd land
  I know a bliss all baser hours deny.
My spirit in his region breathes an air
  That fires its passion for its needful truth;
Feeling no more its sordid earth-born care,
  It dreams its dream of wished for heavenly youth.
This sensuous world grows bleak from day to day;
Its bloom returns when I his power obey.

XII.

I'd know what does my secret soul contain—
  What love and hate are in my heart concealed—
What thrill or tone each passion may attain—
  All secrets of my soul, I'd have revealed:
I would each source of joy or sorrow learn—
  Open the sweet and bitter founts of life;
By heart and eye, experience I would earn,
  Of life's full yield, inbreathing peace and strife:

I'd know what wakes the music of my soul—
   Its highest, lowest, sweetest, tones can sound—
What all its richest concords can control:
   All needful help, I in his genius found.
His soul breathes forth what I desire to know,
But gives, as well, desire a fiercer glow.

XIII.

Mind craving beauty, nature beauty gives,
   In form and hue, and soul's soft lineament:
Or mind makes beauty, where no beauty lives,
   At nature's will, framing its own content.
But that fair whole, from present eyes concealed,
   Nature may for the waiting future crown,
In scattered parts is only now revealed—
   Parts that in union nowhere yet have grown.
We dream of forms the eye but rarely finds,
   Aglow with beauty, flushing from the soul—
With thinking music clothe ideal minds;
   But heaven-born genius makes these parts a
     whole.
Onward the soul! sweet genius for its guide;
Its hope and help, in genius still abide.

XIV.

Come forth, sweet god, and bring thy fire from
    heaven;
    Thy mother faints, still knowing not her state;
To thee the holy mission has been given,
    To lead her up to meet her glimmering fate.
Raise up her torpid soul to that bright realm
    Which, in thy presence only, she may see;
Guide her still gently, ruling thou the helm;
    She sinks past hope if she lose help of thee.
What more wouldst thou, from gracious Nature ask,
    Than be the saviour of thy earth-bound race?
Accept thy own, and heaven will bless thy task,
    If with true heart thou fill thy glorious place.
She lies benumbed by earth's o'ershadowing might;
Through thee must come celestial fire and light.

XV.

Unresting nature ever seeks to gain
    Her full perfection in all things she makes;
But full success she rarely can attain,
    Conflicting powers barring the course she takes.
One flower has beauty, wanting still perfume;
    One rich in scent, is poor in form and hue;
Some, poor in all, their humble lives consume;
    Some, rich in worth, leave seeming for the true.

Through human life, she still pursues her end—
  With faultless form to clothe the beauteous soul;
All vital powers to this she seeks to bend,
  But still success obeys not her control.
Wit, wisdom, worth, and beauty's potent charm,
Too rarely meet to grace the faultless form.

XVI.

See how with beauty, clothe these fragile flowers,
  As for themselves, they wore their beauteous
    show;
And yet, what heart, owning their gentle powers,
  Grows not the richer as their beauties grow?
Their vesture serves, 'twere sure, some private end,
  Aiding to shape the course their lives pursue;
To glad all hearts, still smiling power they lend,
  Their lives, a pleasure bringing, ever new.
I love them, though no love may be returned;
  Yet unreturned, my love, O how sincere!
Their forms then, softly in my memory urned,
  From winter fled, are still in memory dear:
Teaching us love, they show the heart its wealth;
And loving them, sick hearts regain their health.
  2

XVII.

When I look on these wondrous forms of earth,
    Thinking how soon their loveliness must fade,—
That death foredooms all things of earthly birth,
    I ask why all these changing forms were made.
Does life take form to furnish sport for death ?—
    Assume these beauteous shows that death may
      kill ?
Or do the lives that end in ceasing breath,
    Beyond their own, some unknown end fulfil ?
Are we but links, lengthening a lengthening chain
    Bearing some purpose to its distant goal ?
Or does each life some final purpose gain,
    Though serving still the purpose of the whole ?
Or may life's love, feeding life's blissful flame,
Prove love, itself, is nature's final aim ?

XVIII.

All beauty, to some sense, is ever good ;
    All good is in some beauty ever drest ;
When nature seeks to show her highest mood,
    Her truth, with beauty, does she then invest.
What is not beautiful, we deem untrue,
    Awaiting sure destruction's gnawing tooth ;
The soul, from beauty, ever seeks its due,
    And seeks it ever in the garb of truth.

Is truth, with beauty, not identical?
   Or seems not so, to our dull sense of seeing?
Where beauty lives, there truth must be withal;
   Where truth is absent, beauty has no being.
Forms, thoughts, or acts, to sense or sense of duty,
The soul deems true but as they're things of beauty.

XIX.

Now in the stillness of this summer day,
   By this glad stream, or in yon saddening wood,
Thoughts come that will not, when in crowds I stay,
   Where feed the hearts, that feed on hungering
     food.
Here wake now joys, dead in life's battling field—
   Wake by soft touches on the ear and eye;
Here comes that sweet that thought and fancy yield—
   Those hidden joys, in hidden heart that lie.
In revery's dream the past returns to view,
   The was, and wished for, blending in the stream;
What might, but will not, mingling with the true;
   Life, fancy-blest, flows on a wandering dream:
Now craves my soul, the best that nature gives,
And sees the best that in its nature lives.

XX.

Last night, that gracious privilege was mine,
  (Such sure delight poor fortune seldom gives,)
To see, again, that heaven-nursed genius shine
  With light wherein truth's beauty ever lives.
Dull, plodding Time bears heavy hours away,
  As painful toil creeps on to weary night;
With sullen care we drudge through tedious day
  Led on by distant hope's dim, fitful, light.
But hope's fair promise lends but poor relief;
  The hungering heart still makes its constant cry;
The joys of sense it finds are all too brief;
  No sensual feast, the heart can satisfy.
But genius, with its heavenly light, appears,
And lifts the heart above its groveling fears.

XXI.

In those rare scenes that from her genius grow
  By mimic art, that fancy so bewitches,
Fond nature deigns, with open hand to throw,
  Around her favorite, all her love-sought riches.
The beauties we in isolation find,
  That with their single force, the heart inspire,
Here in sweet harmony are all combined,
  And melt the heart with their united fire:

Then nature's boon we take from nature's hand,
  And from her bounty, learn her full intent;
O'er all her children's heart she seeks command,
  By truth and beauty's fair embodiment:
Of pitying grief—of smiles and tears beguiled,
In wondering love, we bless her favorite child.

XXII.

Those scenes of love, of life's reality,
  Illumined by imagination's glow,
Raise high above our poor mortality
  The deathless hope the heart exults to know.
The latent love that sleeps in smouldering hearts,
  Whose heat is quenched by uncongenial strife,
But feels the force that nature's fire imparts,
  Then springs, at once, to pure celestial life.
O love! thou boundless power! o'er all omnipotent!
  All nature's source—thou universal soul!
Still, unconfined by natures wide extent—
  From thee, life, and its sweets, we claim the whole:
And still thine all-resistless power to prove,
Here comes thy child, to tune all hearts to love

XXIII.

She looks with art—with art she speaks and moves—
 And yet how artless is her artfulness;
Nature, in her, shows what she dearly loves;
 Through her, she smiles on those she deigns to bless.
We see the mirthful truth of girlish life—
 The love and tenderness of woman shown;
Faith and affection grace the wedded wife;
 We see the heart, love's fancy makes its own.
All tender moods that melt the heart to tears,
 And airy joys that mix those tears with smiles,
And wistful hopes that wait on trembling fears,
 Attend her call, through nature's simple guiles.
Her beauty, wit, and heart-born sentiment
Give form and voice to nature's full intent.

XXIV.

Those passions nature to the heart has lent,
 Pictured in outward form, we seek to view—
Their height and depth--each tone and lineament--
 We seek the counterfeit and find the true.
All those that in the heart of woman glow—
 Love, jealous doubt, and tearful injured pride—
A murmured tone, or look, or gesture show
 How deep their homes within her breast abide.

A tone gives meaning to some tender tale ;
    A simple look shows arch simplicity ;
A word and gesture o'er our hearts avail
    To prove, with nature, deep complicity:
All feelings hid in nature's deep recess,
With nature's grace,through her,their forms express.

XXV.

If in my lines, perchance, you find offence,
    And I, in vain, your favor seek to win,
I may, most justly, urge in my defence,
    That you alone were prompter of my sin.
My guiltless pen safe in oblivion lay,
    And there would still have lain through endless
        night,
Had not your genius tempted it to stray,
    Hoping it might some thing of worth indite.
When strikes the quickening flame that genius gives,
    With kindred fire it stirs the torpid soul;
The fire yours gave, still in my nature lives;
    And still your genius does my pen control:
But if too boldly I your smile demand,
Such sins, in future, cease at your command.

XXVI.

Those 'witching dreams that haunt my rural hours,
　　Oft claim they ought in outward form appear;
But still to clothe them, doubt denied all powers,
　　Till your sweet fire had killed my deadening fear.
With unsought fancies thronging on my mind,
　　Feigned persons come, making my thoughts their
　　　　own;
Then suited actions in fit scenes combined,
　　Are wildly on imagination thrown.
Daring presumption then assays the task
　　To give my wild and formless fancies shape—
Flattering I might e'en your approval ask,
　　Till whispers doubt, " Can you her scorn escape?"
Ah, should your favor such a grace concede,
Then has my labor earned its dearest meed!

XXVII.

Forgotten lines, again she has recited,
　　In tones that made my startled spirit thrill;
Words, bare of beauty, still my soul delighted;
　　Though dead before, they charm my memory still.
Till toned by her, they slept all unregarded;
　　Or as tuneless ballads coldly were perused:
Their barren thoughts, being by her reworded,
　　A soul not theirs is through their form transfused.

I gave them form, she gave them life and spirit;
  I gave the organ, she the music brought;
Henceforth, what worth, for me, they may inherit,
    They knew not till her tongue had tuned my
      thought:
Their charm, though fading from their natal hour,
They now resume, with tenfold native power.

XXVIII.

All wrapped in throbbing silence, sit the crowd;
  Keen expectation peers from every eye;
No sound is heard, but hearts that speak aloud;
  Or as they ease their burden with a sigh :
A beauteous form moves on the mimic scene ;
  Her voice comes melting on the stilléd air;
All hearts are hushed, as 'twere a fairy seen ;
  But mine drinks in delight none else can share.
My thoughts return, as memory'd gained a voice,
  But with a new delicious music fraught:
My words returning make my heart rejoice
  As if an angel's tongue respoke my thought.
Feeling and thought, that fired my heart and brain,
With doubled joy, her voice sends home again.

XXIX.

Is yon a dream-form 'mongst the trees before me?
   Or does her music thrill my waking ear?
What sweet enchantment can it be, thrown o'er me?
   And this sweet trembling, comes it all from fear?
All objects near me hold their wonted forms;
   These sounds are truly answered in my mind;
Their threatening discords, too, my heart alarms;
   In dreams all senses are not so combined.
No; 'tis no dream that's rushing through my heart,
   A dream could not so swell it with delight;
To dreams, what power such rapture could impart,
   Or move my heart so with love's heavenly might?
'Tis love that puts enchantment in my eyes,
Showing a bliss a mocking fate denies.

XXX.

I love May morning's tender, dewy light,
   Still evening's ruddy flame upon the hill;
I love the gentle, silent, queen of night,
   Whose pale, sad, smiles, night-haunted valleys fill;
I love the birds when warbling in the wood,
   That lone one most, that charms night with her
     voice;
Sweet breathing flowers, glassed in the rippling flood,
   Add nature's smile, to make my heart rejoice.

All nature's harmony enchants my soul,
  And sets love's thought upon my spirit's wings;
But now my passion she does so control,
  That, loving her, I love all baser things:
Yet in her love there lives such fatal might,
Its smile or frown makes nature's day or night.

XXXI.

Ranging the woods and painted meadows through,
  I gather flowers that spangle summer's green;
But when I would their differing beauties view,
  One constant image does their beauties screen.
I would be studious in wise nature's book,
  And strive to scan some deeply worded page;
But memory turns my eye, with inward look,
  To what does solely memory's love engage.
I hear the birds sing in their leafy home;
  I smell the flowers that breathe around my feet;
But from their presence still does fancy roam,
  And bring new sweetness to their sweetest sweet.
When she's away, her image seals my sight;
When she is near, I see with heavenly light.

XXXII.

In dewy morn of soft and balmy spring,
    When joyous youth makes jocund, early day—
When flowers glad incense to young morning bring,
    How sweetly glide joy-laden hours away!
All beauties strewn o'er Nature's wide domain,
    That feed the eye and ear with pure delight,
With gentle force o'er our affections reign,
    Or quell the heart, with awe-inspiring might.
In Nature's home, I still hear memory's voice,
    Rewording thoughts—recalling every tone—
Her looks recalled, then, make my heart rejoice,
    And make all Nature's beauties seem her own:
No beauty, Nature to the world can give,
But those my heart sees in her being live.

XXXIII.

But how I love, love gives no leave to say,
    Nor trusts its secret to a babbling pen;
And should my love fall on the ear of day,
    'Twould hear but mock'ry from all envious men.
My love brooks not the hard promiscuous gaze
    That scathes not love, of hard, promiscuous life;
Though envy 're sweet, her name in vulgar praise,
    From vulgar tongues, but fills my heart with strife.

With jealous care I then my love conceal—
　　Its treasure hide deep in my secret breast;
How sweet its store, still could no tongue reveal,
　　Even could my heart betray its cherished guest.
Her smile assured, nought else my heart would crave;
But waiting fear, alone, my heart must have.

XXXIV.

The something her's, I must so much admire,
　　That ever makes my heart leap from its seat,
Still turns my soul to one fierce sad desire,—
　　To feverish hope, then doubting, shivering heat.
All tongues attest that she's of lovely form;
　　Of others, perhaps, some tongues attest the same;
Some hearts may find elsewhere a grace as warm;
　　In mine none else can raise so sweet a flame.
My love feeds not on favors she has shown,
　　Nor on the hope of favors she may show;
No smile of kindness has my passion known;
　　Still does my passion keep its constant glow.
In all but her, some thing appears amiss;
In her, has nature crowned each sovereign bliss.

XXXV.

How weak my soul till I did worship thee!
   Still vainly struggling for an upward flight;
Nor till my eye did thy perfection see,
   Ere knew my heart the force of beauty's might.
When sun-beams warm to life the opening flower,
   It breathes its perfume on the evening air;
When to my soul thy spirit yields its power,
   It thinks in forms, its thought exults to wear.
What once were passions fouled with earthy mire—
   Thoughts winged, still clinging to their native
      clay—
Now strengthened by thy beauty's heavenly fire,
   Raise up my soul to meet a heavenly day.
Ah! wilt thou smile on earth perennial bloom?
Or, frowning, shut me in perpetual gloom?

XXXVI.

Long has my heart from hope to fear been tost;
   Had I her love? I hoped, yet feared to know:
But by a look, to-day, all fear I lost—
   A look that set love's hopeless fire aglow.
I saw her smile as she was passing near—
   A dreaming smile, brightening her wandering eye;
And in her smile there hung a trembling tear;
   And with the tear, there came a struggling sigh.

Are gentle sighs, alone the signs of grief?
   Grief-burthened hearts, then, do they always prove?
No; tears may bring love-laden hearts relief,
   And gentle sighs oft ease excess of love.
Her quivering lip and tear-dewed eye proclaim
That in her heart, there lives a love-born flame.

XXXVII.

My burning passion still I must conceal;
   Ev'n from her presence must I still refrain;
More and more hopeless is the love I feel,
   Yet with love's hope, dies not my hopeless pain.
I seek by day a nightly solitude,
   To nourish thoughts that nurture most the soul;
But thoughts of her, all other thoughts exclude;
   Not I, but she, my thinking does control.
And sleepless fancy, in the dreamful night,
   Still shows her image set in airy bliss;
Then in sleep's world I taste love dream's delight,
   But with the day comes back the world that is:
In crowd or solitude, by night or day,
A hopeless love, my joyless heart must sway.

XXXVIII.

I, in the crowd, have seen her once again!
   Oh, were she to all rival eyes unknown!
I freeze, joining the gaze of lickerish men;
   My heart would have her beauty all its own.
Still must I look, and yet to look is pain;
   I turn away; to turn away is grief;
Once more I force my eyes to look again;
   Once more I shift my eyes to find relief.
Were but her beauty to my heart confined,
   All other treasure would it gladly give;
In her, my heart its only heaven would find,
   And there would pray, eternally to live.
So does her gentle power my soul enthrall,
That in her smile, my soul secures its all!

XXXIX.

The prayer bell tolls; the sun now seeks his bed;
   The crimson clouds shut out retiring day;
Venus, awake, smiles through the filmy red
   Dyed in the dying sun's last wandering ray.
And while the moon's full flood of saddening light
   Flows in still silence o'er the shadowy plain,
The timid stars peep from the cave of night,
   And gem the dome that spans the heavenly main.

The drowsy cuckoo's husky, faltering, voice,
  Sleepily comes now through the darkening air,
Bidding me in my twilight hour rejoice,
  Though none be near my twilight hour to share.
A bliss how heavenly! might this hour impart,
Were it but shared by her glad trembling heart!

XL.

'Twas thy blest power that showed me what I am—
  Called forth a sense that else had been concealed;
This blissful passion still were sleeping flame,
  Had'st thou, my soul not to itself revealed.
As lifeless strings that skilful hands control,
  To make soft tremblings in a lifeless air,
A new emotion wake within my soul,
  And plant a joy that else had ne'er been there:
So dost thou, by thy being's beauteous show,
  An unknown power within my spirit prove,
And make my heart that tender suffering know,
  That slept, till thou didst prove my power to love.
From this dear pain my heart was still secure,
'Till taught by thee what thrill it might endure.
  3

XLI.

Why not my soul with thine forever blend,
　As music's sweet concordant sounds unite?
Or why, my heart, 'gainst thy sweet power defend?
　Or thine withhold its love in my despite?
I love thee for that pitiless loveliness,
　That, while thou art, compels me still to love;
Thy loving owns 'all power my life to bless,
　And will till death my love of love remove.
As rose and woodbine, blending their perfume,
　Breathe in delicious union through their day,
In quenchless love, so might our lives consume,
　Nor fear, in time, our love would e'er decay.
My heart loves not, obedient to my will;
While thou art thou, my heart must love thee still.

XLII.

You will not wed? then is your life a sin,
　Robbing the world of its most rare perfection—
Ending a race where one you might begin,
　If nature's will you gave the true direction.
All human souls, would nature clothe with beauty,
　Though from her purpose, oft constrained to
　　swerve;
To serve her aim, all then should deem a duty,
　And her best gifts should duteously preserve.

See nature now, gracing unsparing Time
   With one true master-work of her production!
And you, then, guilty of the wasteful crime
   Of leaving Time to work its sure destruction.
Let present eyes enjoy it while they may,
But let its copies grace a future day

LXIII.

Winter retreats, and comes the blessed spring,
   Robing anew with Time's most fragrant glory—
Beckoning with smiles each dear consenting thing
   To glad her hours with mute or tuneful story.
The gentle primrose bares her modest face;
   The air enriched, declares the violet near;
The daisy smiles up from his humble place,
   To greet the rose, the best-loved of the year.
The welcome black-bird, from the echoing grove,
   Sings mated love is sweetener of his song;
The mateless cuckoo shouts, Even vagrant love
   Proves life for life, to nature does belong:
All living things would Nature's wish obey,
And leave their heirs, when they by time decay.

XLIV.

O fairest form that nature yet has made!
    Thou richest vesture of her richest soul!
Alas! that Time has power to make thee fade,
    And none may Time's relentless hand control!
How weakly does that merely pictured face
    Express those features pictured on my heart!
Their sweetness there, no angel-hand could trace;
    How hopeless, then, all merely human art!
I still in love and trembling worship gaze
    On that sweet, lifeless, product of man's skill;
But if my love, art's faltering hand might raise,
    Then might that hand, my heart's sweet dream
      fulfill.
But as those features in my memory live,
'Tis past all hope, an outward form to give.

XLV.

I've crossed the sea—seen something of a storm,
    Perhaps not the worst, and yet we thought it rough;
The weak ones drowned their tears in their alarm;
    The stoutest owned its rage was quite enough.
The huge ship, where a thousand souls were freighted,
    A helpless thing in blazing gulphs now hung;
She then rolled o'er, as if she'd ne'er be righted,
    While maddening waves against her sides were
      flung.

The night was dark,the tumbling ocean black—
　　Still blacker for the lightning's blinding flash;
We now stood on a bursting mountain's back,
　　Anon down rushing with a shrivering crash.
The wind and ocean drowned the thunder's roar;
Those prayed for help,who seldom prayed before.

XLVI.

Ah! now she sinks! Death stands within the hour!
　　There goes jib-boom, and tears away the mast!
The wind and ocean blend their utmost power:
　　She sinks! O Heaven! Of earth we've seen the
　　　last.
Beneath the hissing foam, the vessel rushes
　　Like some mad creature seeking instant death;
The sea sweeps o'er, and boat and cabin crushes—
　　"All now is o'er!" is gasped in quivering breath.
The moments swell; but none of hope dare think;
　　And death's sure coming seems to all an age;
She lifts her head; but she will backward sink!
　　How weak man's might to cope with nature's rage!
In moments, now, each counts his flickering life;
Even hope is numbed, beneath this deadening strife.

XLVII.

But now she rests a moment on her side,
   As pondering what her foes have power to do;
But with fierce roar, still comes the heaven-kiss'd
    tide,
   Whirling a crest fringed with a fiery blue.
She bravely once more lifts her struggling head;
   The sinews cut, she drops a shattered wing;
Though rolling wildly on her treacherous bed,
   She still defies all power her foes can bring.
Our straining hearts, unhoping, pray for life,
   And pray the brave thing's foes their war may
    cease;
But still unpitying, roars death-threatening strife;
   And still white lips pray heaven for quick release.
But time still moves, and darkness creeps away;
'Tis some relief to meet our fate by day.

XLVIII.

The sun is up; the wind has spent his force;
   But the still angry sea is rolling high;
All sail is set; we're speeding on our course,
   When "overboard," "man overboard," they cry.
All hear the cry; the rush to help is brisk;
   All fly at once to where the cry is heard;
To save this life, the men are wild to risk
   Those lives the forespent storm 'till now had spared.

A piercing cry comes up above the din;
　With desperate hope the man still rides the wave;
"The boat!" The boat, alas! is found stove in;
　No means are left the struggling man to save.
All lives are safe the storm had doomed to death;
This death has doomed, though still we hear his
　　breath.

XLIX.

I saw his look as he was rushing by,
　His 'wildered soul, death-startled, in his face;
I heard his frantic, fierce, imploring cry:
　Time will not soon the saddening sight efface.
He sunk a moment, then he rose once more;
　His harrowing cry, again still'd wave and wind;
He sunk and rose, but we sped on before;
　The flying ship soon left him far behind.
All eyes were strained, to catch a final glance;
　Some saw him still, when he had surely gone;
That death, that seemed last night our only chance,
　Had passed the rest, and seized on him alone.
Those hearts Death's threats, so late, had shook with
　　fear,
Forgot the past, now Death had struck so near

L.

The poor, reluctant soul had burst the screen
    That stands between what must be and what is;
He clung, with frenzy, to this transient scene,
    As if to woe he went, from scenes of bliss.
Not he alone betrays such frantic fear
    To meet a fate no breathing thing may shun;
But few say, truly, when such fate comes near,
    "Not mine, Dread Power, but thy good will be
      done."
We may not wonder such untimely fate
    Should so this unprepared soul affright;
He knew his present—not his future state;
    He left the day, to plunge in seeming night.
He trusted solely in the life now ending;
No faith had he, a future life was pending.

LI.

But should that death that must to life succeed,
    As sleepful night succeeds the wakeful day—
That death that is with life itself decreed,
    Have that dark power that shakes us with dismay?
To shun sure death, the saddest will endeavor;
    While life has hope, death ever comes too soon;
Though all would live, yet who would live forever,
    And deem unending earthly life, a boon?

May we not make this life a thing of beauty
 To be perfected in this frame of dust,
And graft a future joy on present duty,
 Then on life's ending look without distrust?
Though death we view as nature's angry frown,
Had death been wrong, this life had ne'er known

LII.

But, fearing death, do I spend fear in vain?
 And is death stayed till some set task be done?
And, though death-doomed, must I still here remain
 Till all peculiar in my life is shown?
Though weighty tasks to strong hands are assigned,
 Great issues oft through weak ones may descend;
Fate's purpose being not to the great confined,
 Even such as I may serve some purposed end.
Yet what fit purpose can my life fulfil,
 For which ever-nearing Death that life must spare?
And, as Death's hand, does fate control my will,
 To make some special end my special care?
The bee sips honey, and the beetle gnaws;
I serve a general, perhaps a special cause.

LIII.

Few hungering years we wander here on earth,
    Though on what errand sent we are not told;
Mad hopes and passions hurl us on from birth,
    Till withering time has left us drear and cold.
Yet in life's storm-vexed dream a summering lies,
    Wherein that fruitage of time's seasoning grows,
That sweetly stores our hope-sought paradise,
    Or turns to poison, feeding future woes.
The past, to future does its coloring give;
    All actions dying, die to live again;
And sin must burn, yet burning still must live,
    While sin's foul dross does in the soul remain;
As future plant, in sleeping seed abides,
In buried life our living future hides.

LIV.

You hate your life, and crave an endless sleep;
    To force you into life, you deem unjust;
In this vile world you would no longer creep;
    But sink all conscious life in lifeless dust.
Why should we death with such fierce passion crave,
    As if death could some want of life supply?
No healthy heart seeks physic from the grave;
    We're sick, indeed, when we can wish to die.

But you arraign the power that gave you life ;
   Why not condemn what turns that life to ill ?
Those untamed, unfed wants that breed your strife,
   And take their power from your untempered will.
Peace leaves us when we seek a lawless aim :
To win her back, wild passion we must tame.

LV.

Our conscious life is but the spirit's action,
   The soul's fierce conflict with opposing forces—
A conflict yielding still its satisfaction
   But as the spirit drains its life's resources.
Yet varying action does the spirit need;
   Unchanging sameness does the spirit weary;
If on one dish alone the soul must feed,
   Then may its home, indeed, become most dreary.
Life is action; still life's calls are ever changing;
   We suffer as its calls we disregard;
With fixed heart, and fancy widely ranging,
   The spirit ever seeks its just award.
Life still has joys, if we would seek aright;
But joy we find not in stalled appetite.

LVI.

We find not life what we would life should be,
    Nor make we life what we have power to make it;
We boast of eyes, refusing power to see,
    And starve in plenty, wanting will to take it.
We vaunt the hour when sumptuously we dine,
    Despising gods, that must forego their dinner;
If, tricked in state, to envious eyes we shine,
    We mock all different life, of saint or sinner.
So ranked and stalled, with such gross feeding fed,
    The world can serve our souls no higher uses;
Or to all higher use, our souls are dead—
    Dead by long fast, or by past foul abuses:
The soul's best needs, we flout from day to day,
Then murmur when life's later joys decay.

LVII.

Again the sun comes from the joyous South,
    Bringing glad Spring from under Winter's shade;
He smiling comes, to kill some joy of youth:
    Each visit now some bloom of life must fade.
The poet's tuned for me his most harmonious verse;
    The sweetest singer's sung his sweetest song;
I've heard the sage his grandest theme rehearse—
    Seen fairest forms that painter's fancy throng.

I've Nature's cunning traced from form to form ;
　　She's shown me what she deems her true and good ;
For me she's wrapped the world in fiery storms ;
　　With smiles she blessed me in her blandest mood.
But man and nature less and less surprise ;
With each new thrill, some expectation dies.

LVIII.

When with fresh youth we breast the hill of life,
　　The heart bounds up with energy and hope ;
To gain some distant prize we wade through strife,
　　As if 'twere sport, with obstacles to cope.
We win the prize that fancy sought, perchance ;
　　An hour exult, then, o'er mad youth's success ;
But youth departs ; hope can no more advance ;
　　Even victory does hope's future scope repress.
We now descend, but with reverted view ;
　　The joy we sought, lies lifeless in the past ;
With faltering heart, we distant aims pursue,
　　Knowing each sun falls still more near the last :
But still the heart is by illusion fed ;
And thus through life, we're by delusion led.

LIX.

But must true life be not, then, held a boon?
  We know its worth when we know how to live;
Its needs change not with changes of the moon,
  Yet each new day should have new joy to give.
In love alone we find our source of bliss;
  And as we love, we do life's blessings know;
Those who love not, life's true enjoyment miss,
  And so life's dearest object must forego.
Those things we love—that feed the craving heart—
  When we their needed presence may possess,
If wholesome joy alone they do impart,
  Bring all we need, to make life's happiness.
In boundless love, there lives a boundless joy;
But this poor life does not such love supply.

LX.

I hate, and yet I may not state the cause;
  I hate, and yet my hate I may not vent;
A hate unceasingly within me gnaws,
  And still it must within my heart be pent.
I know my hate a curse, and yet I hate;
  I hate, and yet I know the bliss of love;
If thinking might my gnawing curse abate,
  Then thinking might, in time, my curse remove.

But hate, with thought, comes like a heated knife,
   And, like a flame, strikes through my poisoned
      heart;
My reason holds with hate a bootless strife ;
   In vain, my reason bids my hate depart.
Of hatred's folly, I can reason well ;
And yet my hatred makes my heart a hell.

LXI.

But when I love, I know that I am blest—
   That with my hate there ever comes a curse ;
In love alone my heart would ever rest,
   Yet will my heart its cause of hatred nurse.
A snake, I madly in my bosom cherish,
   Knowing full well the danger of its fangs—
Nurse it again to life, knowing must perish
   All inward peace, with hatred's deadly pangs.
I'm mad, I know, to cherish hatred so,
   While what I love this hatred will destroy—
To quench the thought that makes affection glow,
   And seize a curse where I might have a joy.
But such is rooted passion's peevish course,
It seeks a blessing from a cursed source.

LXII.

I love: though I may not my love reveal,
    I know the joy 'twould bring to make it known;
Like scent, that roses in their hearts conceal,
    In secret sweet, 'twere sweeter being shown.
With love there comes a peace that feeds the spirit;
    Love ever brings the heart its sweetest health;
How blest are those who do the power inherit
    To force the world to yield such heavenly wealth.
Love comes with thought, and with a thought will go;
    By fancy's light, my heart does treasure find;
Not by mere reason's, but imagination's glow,
    My heart's best fruits are ripened in the mind.
If, then, in love the heart finds surest rest,
Might reason ask, "Why not be always blest?"

LXIII.

Love smiles on nature, from glad summer's source,
    And straight she clothes herself in tender green—
With dearest music, joys the summer's course,
    Leaving her flowers where her soft touch has been.
And still exulting in the smile of love,
    Though passing now the summer's fervid glow,
Her flowery bounty would she now improve,
    And leave rich fruits where she but set their show.

But winter meets her, with his hideous frown,
　　And o'er her heart breathing his deadening breath,
Straight are love's gifts of joy and bounty flown,
　　And nature, naked, sinks in shivering death:
So joy we know, as love smiles on the heart;
At hate's fierce touch, from life all joys depart.

LXIV.

These wondrous shows that on our vision rise
　　We view as children faded baubles view;
And hourly see with dull unwondering eyes
　　Life's boundless source pour forth life ever new.
Yon flaming orb that floods the heavens with light,
　　And rescues nature from eternal sleep—
The moon that with soft silver bathes the night—
　　The stars that float across yon boundless deep—
The flash that wraps the rolling clouds in flame—
　　The radiant bow that spans the parting shower—
We in dead, cold, familiar accents name,
　　As things unnoted in each passing hour.
As nature serves us, nature we respect;
We see no gods where we no gain detect.

4

LXV.

The day is bright; the sun is soaring high;
  The leaves are gently playing in the air;
At every step, rejoicing meets the eye,
  As if the day could find no room for care.
Life, like the day, appears now at its noon,
  The birds and flowers proclaiming general gladness;
To live, now seems to all a joyous boon;
  No heart now deems there may be future sadness.
But stop! what's that, that does life's current freeze?
  Stark death, and in his most appalling shape!
A suicide, who sought beneath these trees,
  From hopeless life, in hopeless death escape.
He, though no felon, as a felon dies;
To kill his woe, the hang man's rope he tries.

LXVI.

An hour ago he bore that form upright
  That sets man proudly at creation's head;
Now there he lies, that horrid, sickening sight:
  To such an end, has vaunted reason led.
Should reason so set man below the beast?
  While instinct's sure, should reason lead astray?
Should reason curse creation's plenteous feast,
  While instinct makes its life a festal day?

'Tis even so—'tis sad it should be so—
   That thus life's conflict should so often end ;
Men who with angels might aspire to go,
   How often thus below the brute descend.
That ghastly wreck, where dwelt one of my race,
Now seems a fiend's deserted dwelling place.

LXVII.

This darkling soul, on fate's wild stream has tost
   O'er shallow joys, deep grief, and turpid care;
Now hope gave light: anon all light is lost,
   Till madly ending here, in fierce despair.
Drifting with chance, unwitting of life's chart,
   He sought the boon that all in life would find;
Impelled by gustful passion from the heart,
   His way unseen, in twilight of the mind.
Now wild, unchastened, hopes his fancy fill;
   Untempered lusts then scorch him in their deeds;
But now his fierce desires have had their will,
   How cold and joyless are his wintry needs.
He proved the chance that fate to man has given,
To find a hell where he expected heaven.

LXVIII.

Such wrecks might stand as beacons to our view,
    And show the tempters on life's common way—
Signal the course we recklessly pursue,
    Whose ending, here we look on with dismay.
The light that led him, loadstars every soul;
    Through mental fog, he sought what all would
        gain;
He failed; and here before this desperate goal,
    Hope died; death now seemed death to endless
        pain.
He took for guide, his untamed appetite;
    He gave to passion all he had to give;
He heeded not that nature does requite
    With curses, all who for mere passion live.
He fiercely seized all joys that he could borrow;
But with the joys he seized a deadly sorrow.

LXIX.

Did he bear leave from nature's source of life
    To end his course by rash felonious hand?
Might he, still blameless, quit his post of strife,
    Still unfulfilled his sovereign's full command?
We hang in time like fruit on forest trees,
    And into time by sovereign power are sent,
To bear all summer suns and wintry breeze,
    Till we have drained all seasons' nutriment.

Untimely death defeats life's destiny;
   Lives miss their due, that do untimely end;
Nor fruit nor flowers their full perfection see,
   That on untimely chances do depend.
Even this poor life, we see untimely ended,
Had surely been by timely sufferance mended.

LXX.

He's now, the poor misdeeming soul, at rest;
   He's found, too sure, how vain is vanity;
With all who trust mere noise can bring the best,
   He's found, at last, his hope's inanity.
All toil was cheap, that brought him noisy fame,
   And set his name afloat on vulgar breath;
If but a foolish few might shout his name,
   Peace had no price—no terror hastening death.
Not "It is well," but "That men deemed it so,"
   A moment slaked his thirsting heart's desire;
All sense of just and true, that rage could quell,
   That fed his peaceless heart with quenchless fire.
But blame for praise! how worthless life was then!
Such worthless worth he gave to breath of men.

LXXI.

When few more years with ruthless Time have flown,
   And swept their due from unresisting space,
This all I now so fiercely call my own,
   In Time's sad ruin then must have its place:
When those dead years that in my memory lie,
   In future's womb concealed their changeful,
There, too, was hid this self-regarding I,
   That loves and hates now in a conscious life.
I am that was not; soon I shall not be—
   A life enduring while some god might wink—
A dewdrop, hanging in immensity,
   Wresting from sunbeams power to feel and think.
Soon must the force that could insphere a soul,
Again remerge into a lifeless whole.

LXXII.

Few years ago this spirit had no being,
   Or as now clothed it then had ne'er been seen;
To realms unknown, again 'tis ever fleeing,
   To be or not, as it had never been.
But for earth's turmoil must it come and go—
   Be tossed an hour in storms of thought and feeling?
A conscious actor be, to feel and know,
   Its body's end, its being then repealing?

Or does some unseen power this dust control,
  To start a life not on this dust depending?—
From lifeless matter, form a deathless soul,
  With body growing, not with body ending?
But as it should, so will it surely be;
Who gave this life, its future can decree.

LXXIII.

Whence, earth-sojourning spirit, hast thou come?
  Thy sojourn ended, whither art thou going?
Wilt thou, as weeds, thy cradle make thy tomb?
  Or elsewhere reap what mortal hours are sowing?
Thou'rt blest in time—or curst—with consciousness;
  Thou'st power to say, "In time and space I am;"
Knowing, per force, that power thou dost possess,
  Thou know'st no whence or why that power be-
    came.
Of nature's powers, thou say'st thou art compact,
  Converging forces blending in thy being;
But so inferring nature's power to act,
  Leaves still unknown the prior power decreeing.
Thy whence or why, all nature's power conceals;
Thy hence or how, what greater power reveals?

LXXIV.

But does the soul that moves this sentient dust,
   In this brief hour its destined end attain?
Or may we ask if such a fate were just,
    While threatening death stings life with trembling
      pain?
All living things bear nature's fatal hand,
   And ever upward is their vital law;
All yield obedience to the stern command,
   Or feed destruction's ever hungry maw.
The law swerves not at man's humanity;
   The power supreme o'er all he must obey;
Yet, does this round of earth's inanity
   Inclose man's final hour of conscious day?
Unaided sense no other fate can see;
Hope cries, "No, no, such fate can never be."

LXXV.

When winter flies before all-gladdening spring,
   And May's sweet smile again on earth is thrown,
Warming to life and joy each sleeping thing,
   With what full heart we make spring's joy our
     own.
But thou, brief life, by thy dear advent brought
   Joy, else unknown, and life-long promised bliss—
Dear hope unhoped for, and before unsought,
   Now hope no more, killed by death's freezing kiss.

My stainless snowdrop, blooming one bright hour,
  With summer's hope blessing the sweat of toil,
Now breathed on by dread death's all-mastering
    power,
  Its fading does life's fruitful hours despoil :
In thee death does my life's new hope destroy,
And plant a grief where thou hadst planted joy.

LXXVI.

To me, then, art thou now forever dead,
  If all thou wert, death had the power to kill—
Forever, now, that budding hope is fled,
  That thou life's future sweetest hours would'st fill.
The quickening love, woke by thy opening smile—
  The pitying tears, touched by thy tearless wail—
With fruitless hope, do now my heart beguile,
  If nought of thee might o'er death's power prevail.
Though thou art dead, love sprung from thee still
    lives,
  And as life fades, still does the stronger grow;
Fed by—feeding—the hope the future gives,
  What death forbade I in the past should know :
A hope still sings that death has been defeated—
That where death reigns not thou wilt be completed.

LXXVII.

And she, few months ago, that said good-bye,
    With laughing heart of blooming, buoyant youth,
Saying, in jest, " No more she'd glad my eye,"
    Speaking, how mirthfully, the saddest truth.
In random phrase, of life and death we spoke ;
    Life seemed secure ; we deemed not death was
        near ;
But now, in grief, sad memory hears the joke ;
    Where we could laugh I now must drop a tear.
Those hearts now mourn, her presence once made
        glad ;
    And all were glad that in her presence came ;
But death has killed the joy her presence had ;
    Grief comes alone, whene'er we speak her name.
But heavenly peace go with thee ever more !
We come thy way ; thou art but gone before.

LXXVIII.

Time drifts me once more from my wonted place,
    Rending the ties by which my heart is bound,
Proving once more that in life's changing phase,
    For me, in change, not joy, but grief is found.
Where grows the tree, there would it ever grow;
    There can its rootlets find life's nutriment ;
To tear it whence life's needful succors flow,
    Still brings its life injurious detriment.

My heart from things familiar gathers life ;
   O'er scenes it loves, it would forever range ;
All change it owns, must come from outward strife ;
   Where still it loves, it ne'er would seek for change.
But time moves on, and outward conflict brings,
Tearing the heart from loved familiar things.

LXXIX.

Where loves the heart, there would it ever live,
   Though change, alone, may satisfy the mind;
What gives new thought, the mind new life can give;
   But in time's change, no life the heart can find.
We see, to-day, what we have seen before;
   We heed it not, but ask for something new;
Anon we find what adds to memory's store,
   The craving mind then claims its needful due.
New objects only, bring the mind new thought;
   Old objects only, bring the heart new life;
Mind's ceaseless growth, from ceaseless change is
     wrought;
   The heart finds only death, in ceaseless strife:
The mind through boundless nature seeks to range;
Through boundless time, the heart would never
     change.

LXXX.

To-day, my heart its best of life would know,
    Though deeming, still, life's best in future lies;
But in each hour, still does this craving grow;
    And yet each hour this craving still denies:
Thus mocking hours life's crowning hours postpone,
    But with sweet flattery still persuade the mind
That each poor best that with past hours has gone,
    Leaves some untasted better best behind.
In life's best hour, though sunned in nature's smile,
    Finding life less than all it still expects,
My heart must yield to hope-fed fancy's guile,
    Though fancy's guile, it in that hours detects.
That good, the heart in future hours descries,
From present touch, to hours still future flies.

LXXXI.

The good I chase is ever on the wing;
    When I would seize it, onward it has flown;
Still is my best that ever-fleeing thing,
    That, rainbow-like, is ever distant shown.
Each day finds fancy's scope still more contracted,
    Hope's failures leaving hope's range newly
        bounded;

Each day my heart finds some new cheat enacted,
  Still is its trust on fancy's promise founded.
Yet hope can still sing to a listening ear—
  Her suasive smile draw on my endless chase;
As from my grasp hope's phantoms disappear,
  False fancy still sets new ones in their place:
Dead with to-day, hope still lives with to-morrow;
  Or death were hope, and life a hopeless sorrow.

LXXXII.

Where may be found that full content of life—
  That life's content which true life should afford?
Each passing hour seems with enjoyments rife,
  Yet not with those that with my mood accord.
The joys we have, are turned to discontent
  In craving those that swell another's share;
Content we lose, which wanting we lament,
  When with our own, we happier lots compare.
And, still, should rankling envy be my choice,
  Though I may have not what my neighbor has?
May I not in my poorer joy rejoice,
  Although another's joy my own surpass?
To win such joys as nature has to give,
On what it has, the heart must learn to live.

LXXXIII.

But is the guerdon of my life's endeavor
    Summed in those fruits that fade each fading day?
That feed, yet starve, leaving life hungry ever—
    More hungry still as life's fleet hours decay?
Must life's best hours but tantalize the mind—
    Still bring no joy the heart does not remember?
And, flattering life's true worth is still to find,
    But paint sweet May beyond each day's December?
A spring to have, in having proves a winter;
    The whole possessed, the heart is still defeated;
Still does the heart give hope glad leave to enter,
    Then finds hope's mocking still once more re-
        peated.
But death would nature's living power defeat,
If thou, bland hope, forego thy power to cheat.

LXXXIV.

But still confined within a sunless sphere,
    Where still there comes a wintry discontent,
Dreaming of joys that bloom to suns elsewhere,
    Still hungry yearning in my heart is pent!
And as a bird, love's prisoner in his cage,
    Beating his prison walls to set him free,
Deaf to all voices but that instinct's rage
    That pants for unknown joys beyond the sea:

So would my heart go where that summer lives,
   Flying this winter of a life-long date—
Where blooming hope its promised fruitage gives,
   Changing the mockery of this barren state.
This gloom makes winter of the summer's glow,
And joyless waste where joyous flowers should grow.

LXXXV.

Yet, would we live not in such hours as this?
   Nor deem the power to know their joy a treasure?
Joy that might tune the soul to pressnt bliss,
   And memory store, too, with a future pleasure.
The sun's smile gladdens every leaf and flower;
   The air shakes perfume from his gentle wings;
Heaven's music starts to life in every bower,
   Calling to peace, through every bird that sings:
Unnoted flowers, bestained with every dye,
   From grassy covert, breathe their soft appeal;
Soul-soothing touches come from earth and sky,
   That would all heart distempering discord heal:
But while black discontent beclouds the sight,
Nature may charm, but charm to sour delight.

LXXXVI.

You ask why I so dearly love the past,
    Although its memories touch me with regret?
What joys once o'er my fresh young heart were cast,
    My heart, life-poverished, will not now forget.
Life once was new—no appetite was cloyed;
    Hope told her tale; her tale seemed ever true;
The joys now spent, had once to be enjoyed,
    And hopes now dead had once life ever new.
'Tis not in having, we all pleasure find;
    The hunter finds his pleasure in the chase;
Though tales retold lose power to please the mind,
    The heart may look with love in memory's face;
And more and more, as we approach the end,
Do present joys upon the past depend.

LXXXVII.

My memory still brings back my childhood's time,
    And with it comes an old man and his ass,
Who, when the days were in their sunny prime,
    Murmuring low songs, the silent lanes would pass.
To Fairy-land the old man seemed to go,
    Where slept soft echoes of the cuckoo's song;
Where rose and blue-bell sweeter still should grow,
    Than those that did to nature's world belong.

Oh! what soft yearning filled my childish breast,
   That I the old man's fairy world might see;
Him and his ass my fancy did invest
   With gentle charms, unseen by all but me:
He lived, and still lives, in that summer day,
Which now remembered, winter turns to May.

LXXXVIII.

When in dear spring while daisies still were young,
   And hawthorns hung their mantles on the hedges;
When thrush and ousel thrilled the wood with song,
   And warblers hailed the moon among the sedges;
When joyous life, now freed from winter's arms,
   Had roused her children from his deadening spell;
When flowers threw on the air their fragrant charms,
   And feathered throats with amorous notes would
     swell;
When nature's heart throbbed with connubial love,
   And single hearts with kindred hearts could pair—
I learn't how sweet 'twas with the brook to rove,
   Ere time had dulled young fancy's world with care:
'Twas in that time, when nature could surprise,
With nature's heart, I learn't to sympathize.
  5

LXXXIX.

I sought the poppies hiding in the corn,
 Alone on many a silent summer day;
When on the wings of childish fancy borne,
 My soul would with the birds flee far away:
Then would the lark soar singing o'er my head—
 The cuckoo's voice come from some distant tree,—
The minnows frisk around their rippling bed—
 The breathing clover call the wandering bee:
And while this music still would charm my ear,
 Some gentle pair, perhaps, building in the bush,
Would doubt awhile, then lay aside all fear,
 And twitter love, to break the heavenly hush.
O sweet, how sweet, the memory of that season!
Such joys come not now with the flow of reason.

XC.

Those childish joys will still to memory come,
 And throw their sunshine o'er this dreary now;
From now to then, still will my memory roam—
 With that sweet know not, glad this sad to know.
For memory, bees rob breathing beds of clover,
 Then wing their riches to their distant hoard;
Still, gentle birds hop round the leafy cover
 That hides the dearest joys their lives afford.

The fairy world, I lived in then alone,
   Still fancy frames in summer solitude;
In memory still, it sweetly is my own,
   And now as then, no stranger may intrude.
Those simple joys that filled my heart with pleasure,
In after years, have proved a precious treasure.

XCI.

Life then flowed on in sweet expectancy,
   As purling streams wind through the purple mea-
     dows;
Hope's revery shaping joys that were to be,
   My world, the while, a world of moving shadows
Alone—in heart and fancy still alone—
   My silent haunts, all feet but mine forsook—
For me the wren would pipe his tenderest tone,
   While cowslips softly kissed the loitering brook.
Then memory plucked young fancy's fadeless flowers,
   Which still she cherishes in rich profusion;
Though care may now o'er shade these riper hours,
   Ripe years but make more dear the child's illusion.
To joys then born, the heart still fondly clings,
While those fall dead, that late experience brings.

XCII.

Again the trees put on their autumn glory,
  So changed from that loved garb they donned in
    spring!
But changing hues befit life's changing story,
  And these grace well what autumn hours will
    bring.
Some still their mantles wear of natal green,
  Like hearts still youthful in the breast of age;
Some gray and withered, as if life had seen
  Some blight, that might untimely death presage.
All hues we see, that nature's limners know,
  As yellow, brown, and every tint of red;
While some in all the tones of purple glow,
  As if to vaunt the glorious life now fled.
So rich is nature in her hues and forms,
  Even touched by death, she does but change her
    charms.

XCIII.

Dear Autumn! though thou churlish Winter lead,
  Thy mien more tender, as thou mayst not tarry,
Less loved is Spring, that Winter does succeed,
  Teaching the birds and flowers to woo and marry.
Well does thy sadly sweet, benignant, smile
  Denote those riches all so freely borrow;

But, as a friend that blessed and cheered awhile,
  Thou soon wilt leave us to our winter sorrow.
Gay hopeful Spring, old Winter's deadly foe,
  At Winter's death, proclaims all life is pleasure;
Then fervid Summer brings his sumptuous show;
  But thou art heir to Spring and Summer's treasure.
May I, enriched by Summer hours decease,
But smile like thee, to see my hours decrease.

XCIV.

Ah! oft I stood in childish ecstacy,
  To hear lone Robin's song of mournful gladness!
When yellow leaves hung drooping from the tree,
  No voice but his, moving sweet Autumn's sadness.
Spring's choristers, then silent and forlorn,
  Would eye me mutely in my pensive ramble,
And watch me pluck the haw still on the thorn,
  Or some belated berry from the bramble.
In Robin's pause, the dreaming world was still—
  All but a leaf, perhaps, falling in the bushes;
The Sun, stooping to kiss the distant hill,
  Would flush heaven's face with purple blushes.
I've passed from child to man—from clime to clime;
But autumn still is sweeter for that time.

XCV.

If thy dear song, sweet friend, declare thy heart,
 Rejoice thou art by kindly fate a bird—
That with my own sad fate, thou hast no part
 To lose those joys thy summer hours afford.
Thou, instinct blest, sits singing time away;
 I, reason curst, stop time with boding sorrow;
No woes afflict thee from an unborn day;
 I'm sad to-day, lest I be sad to-morrow.
Thou let'st kind nature for thy wants provide,
 And usest well what nature does supply;
I madly seek what ne'er may be enjoyed,
 And blindly pass the joys that near me lie:
Thou, instinct led, art wise by nature's rule;
I, reason vaunting, am but nature's fool.

XCVI.

Thou tak'st, to-day, all that to-day can give
 Of those sweet joys that to thy life belong;
To-morrow, if to-morrow thou may'st live,
 Thou'lt feed thy heart, then, on to-morrow's song.
But my wise heart is on some pleasure set,
 That comes, if ever, with some distant day,

The passing hour, packing with sour regret,
    Still hoarding hopes that must each hour decay.
Now's hopes, thou hop'st not future hours to view
    As doubling joys that future hours provide;
But taking joys that do each hour accrue,
    Thou fear'st no lack that future hours may hide.
While heart-wrung doubt, my life makes hourly pain,
Thy trusting heart makes life an hourly gain.

XCVII.

Thy song can still recharm my memory back
    To those glad hours when we were young to-
        gether—
And memory charm, too, from that arid track
    That fate has forced me o'er to bring me hither.
But now I meet not that enchanting hue,
    Then o'er life's future thrown by fancy's youth;
No rainbow-light now meets my backward view;
    Now all is truth, how seldom welcome truth!
Thou'rt joyous still, as when at first we met;
    Thy dearest hopes, thou'st found not blank illusion;
But those once in my flattering fancy set,
    Have one by one shown me their sad conclusion:
Thou mov'st me yet, though with a saddening thrill;
So once could men; how few thy power have still.

XCVIII.

I love thee still; but what is that to thee?
　My love or hate gives thee nor joy nor sadness;
But loving thee! how much is that to me!
　Not thine, but my love gives my heart its gladness.
Yet thee I knew not, but alone a voice,
　As 'twere an angel's, quiring in the bushes,
Where thou wilt still to moons of May rejoice
　Long after death my joy and sorrow hushes.
There did'st thou sing sweet summer nights away
　Long ere proud man proclaimed this isle his own;
There wilt thou still sing songs to dearest May
　When my sad race is here no longer known.
Thy youth is constant, while my life is fleeting;
But deathless is the memory of our meeting.

XCIX.

Those speeding years that swept my youth away,
　And bore me hence, in distant lands to roam,
Have left thee still the darling child of May—
　Still in this dear secluded spot at home.
Canst thou, sweet friend, recall one heavenly night,
　A boy thou'dst charmed, and thou were here alone?
And while the moon shed down her sacred light,
　Thou strained'st thy voice, to reach her heavenly
　　throne?

Thou mind'st it not, but I remember it well,
   And of that night, this still my memory nurses:
While wordless thanks to heaven, thy heart could
      swell,
   One speech-endowed, sent heavenward direst
      curses.
Man's voice, profaning night with blasphemy,
Thou would'st have drowned in thankful harmony.

C.

Each day we would some novel pleasure prove,
   Or some old pleasure newly drest would meet;
We seek no pleasure where no more we love;
   But where we love, we pleasure would repeat.
But love dies quickly, if not truly fed;
   Love over fed, yet still more quickly dies;
Time kills the loves that in hot youth were bred;
   But ah! how poorly Time their place supplies.
Now dead, forever dead, that dreaming time
   That made of childhood's day, a summer bliss:
Now dying, too, the hope of passion's prime;
   Now each new day some source of joy I miss.
Life kills the joys that life itself had given;
Then dies the heart, when all life's joys are riven.

CI.

Now, now, and now, still melt into the past,
    Now, heir of now, thrusting now from its place;
Now with a thought, now, too, is onward cast:
    Thus moments run their never ending race.
A thing of now, life so, from stage to stage,
    Each moment adds new distance from its source;
The first of youth leading the last of age,
    Life keeps with time its unrelenting course.
Thought goes with time, and still in memory stays,
    Or memory builds of dead time's thought congealed;
As moments die, each moment's thought decays;
    Yet in new moments, are old thoughts revealed.
Thought, born of time, does all time's power dispute;
Yet thought gives time its one sole attribute.

CII.

I gain, to-day, some object of pursuit,
    Which once I thought my heart might satisfy;
But now that my success has borne its fruit,
    Some further need, does still my heart descry.
Can no success e'er bring full happines?
    Or does not victory always gain the prize?

Or when the prize I sought I may possess,
    Must some new hunger ever thence arise?
The end now gained but shows some further goal
    My still aspiring heart now seeks to gain;
It yields some joy, perchance, but not the whole
    That hope's ambition cries it must obtain.
I may not rest, but onward still must go;
Joys from new conquest, still my heart would know

CIII.

What pleasures can I ever more expect
    Beyond such as I have already tasted?
Can future hours bring pleasures more perfect
    Than those that on the buried past were wasted?
To-day does but some previous day repeat—
    Some story tell, to be re-told to-morrow;
I in new days no novel joys now meet,
    But such as I from bankrupt hope would borrow.
By sated sense our daily joys are bounded;
    In custom's web our feeble lives are fettered;
By rarer joys that on poor hope are founded,
    Our barren days, we find too seldom bettered.
Though hope defraud us still each day we live,
Faith still, each day, to faithless hope we give.

CIV.

Should common joys not keep us from despair?
   With common wants, these ever must recur;
All rarer joys are joys because they're rare:
   To life of common joys, why then demur?
Those fierce delights that can but seldom come,
   Grow cold and stale, being too often sought;
Our dull delights a brighter glow assume,
   If by due fast they be but duly bought.
Our daily needs, our life's true worth increase,
   If well-timed answers meet their hourly call;
With life itself, life's joys can only cease,
   If surfeit do not nature's craving pall.
But wasteful passions bankrupt passion's treasure;
Well-measured loves, life's true enjoyment measure.

CV.

But raging lusts our life's true wealth destroy,
   Then mock us for our joyless poverty;
With gross excess, we nature's craving cloy,
   Then seek delight where no delight may be:
We waste our pleasure's means, with spendthrift
     hand,
   Without such waste our purposed end forwarding;

As oft we miss the joys we might command,
　By wasteful thrift, too much joy's means regarding.
The end we seek, our means but seldom measure;
　We starve to-day for yesterday's excess;
To-day untimely pluck an unripe pleasure
　Which ripely we to-morrow might possess:
We seek our pleasures always out of season;
When passion calls, our souls are deaf to reason.

CVI.

Nay, tempt me not, sweet angel of the fiend!
　I know thy power, know thou that I am weak;
Be not my foe, now seeming so my friend!
　If thou must slay, some willing victim seek.
Thy painted pleasure I must fain forego;
　Thee and my baser self I must resist;
Forbear! work not my nobler self a woe
　That kills me where, alone, I would exist.
My better must my baser self control,
　Or must, itself, of baseness be attainted;
Assail not then, sweet foe, my wavering soul,
　That with sweet sin is but too well acquainted:
'Twixt sense and soul, let me so equipoise,
That future hours may deem the present wise.

CVII.

Again in sin, again with groans repenting!
 Again whirled from my course by passion's might!
One moment raging, in the next relenting;
 Then fiercely wrong, now doing more than right.
But passion blusters; conscience must be still;
 And sleeping conscience, appetite assails;
The brute and beast, one moment have their will;
  The next, roused conscience o'er their power pre-
   vails.
Can this poor soul live out no better plan
 Than this vile hourly change from good to evil?
One moment be all that becomes a man,
 And in the next take promptings from the Devil!
Poor soul indeed! that is in all things double,
From heaven and good flying to sin and trouble.

CVIII.

Two souls I have, or one divided soul;
 One heavenward breathed; one rioting in the
  blood;
'Mongst farthest stars, one would its life enscroll;
 This festering dust gives one its dearest good.
One wings me where true life, indeed, may be,
 And would all memory of my baser blot;

No moment onward, would that baser see,
   Still gluttoning here 'mongst joys that seethe and
     rot.
O, some sweet power my baser self secure,
   And turn its fire to feed my nobler life!
Or must this war 'twixt high and base endure,
   Me still the victim of their torturing strife?
But prayerful hope, on this, at least, may lie:
This flesh being dead, my baser self may die.

CIX.

Rage on, base Wrong, the hour thy fate affords;
   Though now supreme, thou'rt surely doomed to
     die:
Nought helps thee, that with Nature's will accords;
   Thou warr'st with Time, Time not endures a lie.
Thou graspest all that tempts thy gluttonous maw,
   O'er riding ought that bars thy tyrannous will,
But thy fell tooth can not cut through the law,
   That thy fierce life, thy life will surely kill.
Right and thyself against thyself conspire:
   If Right shall live, then die thou surely must;
Right must consume in her quickening fire;
   Or killing Right, thou bends to meet the dust.
Brute, beast and man, can not in union dwell;
Their deathless feud makes their communion hell.

CX.

Whence, baleful Evil, dids't thou gain thy place,
  To mar man's lot, which else had been so fair?
From age to age, thou keep'st an even pace
  With good, that fosters man with heavenly care.
Though fiercely banned, still dost thou fiercely
      flourish,
  Or diest but that thy progeny may live;
Hearts that hate thee, thou compell'st to nourish,
  And give thee life, when death they seek to give.
Whence, protean curse, was thy dark soul derived?
  Has thy fell brood, from man, a separate source?
Or nature's good art thou, of light deprived—
  Essential virtue on an erring course?
Then, partial good sums up man's total evil,
And rifted hearts send forth man's ruthless devil.

CXI.

Grant me, Dread Power! to know what ill I've done;
  Grant I may truly of all ill repent;
Grant me true light where I astray have gone,
  And light my heart when on dark thoughts intent.
Let me forget all wrong my heart has known;
  If not forget, then let my heart forgive;
O'er all my acts, the light of law thrown;
  Grant I may see what life I ought to live.

Thy will, in all things, let me understand;
    The glory of thy kingdom let me see;
Where truth and beauty glow at thy command,
    Grant Thou, that there my sole affection be.
In act and thought, bow me to Thy control;
In loving duty, fix my wandering soul.

CXII.

All bounteous Power! in whom all souls abide,
    How veiled art Thou, from my pondering gaze!
All but Thy law, Thou dost in darkness hide;
    My wondering search, but ends in wondering
        maze.
My link with Thee, no sense of mine can see;
    Yet must my life some end of Thine fulfil;
How weak my purpose, reft of trust in Thee!
    How poor my heart, when wandering from Thy
        will.
But wherefore should so poor a thing as I
    Be less or more in Thy all-seeing sight?
Why on me should Thy dread injunction lie,
    To see my duty in a Heavenly light?
But ever in wise ignorance let me trust
That, with the needful, Thou hast given the just.

6

CXIII.

While still I am, in memory must remain
  Those noisome weeds my wasting moments nour-
    ish;
If good or ill drop seed of joy or pain,
  Though hidden now, it will in future flourish:
While still I am, must live this passing hour,
  To grace or blot the hours that build my life—
Keep fresh the scent of rose or carrion flower—
  Keep green the root of future peace or strife:
While still I am, no thought or act is lost:
  The future from the present ever grows;
A present sin, a future grief must cost;
  From righteous past, all present pleasure flows:
Not death itself, can past and future sever;
While still I am, I am myself forever.

CXIV.

This conscious now, infraught with all the past,
  Must with all future conscious moments blend;
What cloud or sunshine o'er this now is cast
  Must live until all conscious moments end.
Why, then, not make this now a beauteous now,
  If now, in future, I would have look fair?

What substance I would have the future show,
  Must be the substance of this now's affair.
But learn we not, till learning is too late,
  That present act and thought make future being;
We don a garment we must wear with hate—
  Befoul a face the eye is ever seeing:
Too late we learn this teaching, ever true:
A thievish present steals the future's due.

CXV.

Still, though past life have made the present foul,
  So foul with sin it fouler might not be,
If future days may still enlarge the soul,
  Time's addings may from sin's foul dregs be free.
When rock-born streams refresh foul, turbid, lakes,
  Their settling mud still falling more from sight,
A hue more clear and clear their substance takes—
  More free and freely takes the heaven-shed light:
So, may foul memory not be so replaced—
  Black stains grow dim, and more and more from
      view—
O'er loathesome scars, be graceful figures traced—
  Dead, old and false, o'ergrown by sweet and true?
While time endures, what time may we despair
That Time himself, may Time's foul wrongs repair?

CXVI.

Then let my soul a well dressed garden be,
  Where loathsome weeds may have no room to
    live—
Wherein reverted eye may hourly see
  Some beauteous flower that sure delight may give.
Or as a well-played, rich-toned, instrument,
  The richer as it richer music makes,
Which, giving, does its power to give augment,
  Enriched by gifts more than by what it takes.
As nature's self, in unseen time and place,
  Where beauty was not, beauty multiplies;
So may sweet thought, enriching memory's place,
  From buried past, make present beauty rise.
From restless change, in time for ever fleeing,
J would with beauty clothe my spirit's being.

CXVII.

I'd leave some sure memorial of my life—
  Show how this universe has moulded me—
Show scar or trophy of this mundane strife,
  If future eye a thing so small may see.
I would, though weak, be nature's instrument,
  And serve her purpose in my time and place;

I would presume I on life's course am sent,
  To bear some message hence to future days.
Poor I, that breathed not when this tree was planted,
  Stand forth in time as fruitage of the past;
And if through me some needful good be granted,
  Then be my will with nature's purpose cast.
Small nature's need of aught so weak and brief;
But small's the thing that builds the coral reef.

CXVIII.

As sun-dyed drops that paint the evening shower
  Charm with their radiant light the wondering eye;
As those soft pearls that crown the morning flower
  Most sweetly soothe the hearts whereon they lie;
As those foul bells that hang from festering weeds
  Bestain all contact, with contagious mire;
As venomous tears, the envious nettle breeds,
  Set burning blisters, like pale, liquid fire:
So charms, with gladdening beams, this bounteous
    soul;
  To joyful peace, that soothes each neighboring
    heart;
You by their leprous lives the air befoul,
  Or baleful poison to all near impart:
Sweet, wholesome life, some souls have power to
    give;
Some, upas-like, no good can near them live.

CXIX.

Good day, my friend; how do?   Well, what's the
    news?
  You've heard, of course, how Grubb his office won?
Yes; why do people Grubb so much abuse?
  No doubt, some dirty deed the fellow's done.
I've got a cold.   O how the weather changes!
  How're all at home? Brown's wife has got a cough.
From hot to cold, so quick the weather ranges,
  That colds and coughs are plentiful enough.
But how is trade?   I find it rather dull.
  I met with Jones: the fellow's scarcely civil.
Our rash friend, Brooks, has had a heavy pull;
  And Grimshaw's son is rushing to the Devil.
Thus time and temper we consume together,
On coughs and colds and changes of the weather.

CXX.

At dead of night, I'm startled from my sleep:
  A curst musquito's piping in my ear;
He scents my blood; his scent I know he'll keep:
  I'm mad, and not without a touch of fear.
I wait, to find where he intends to pierce;
  His touch is soft; he knows his life is sought;

At length I strike, and with a blow most fierce!
 I miss, of course—I swear—at least in thought.
He's got my blood, and I have got my blow;
 I lose my sleep, and lose my temper too;
Should I but wink, he'll come again I know,
 To drain more blood, and pierce my veins anew.
Why were such puny vampires ever made?
Is curse provoking their infernal trade?

CXXI.

How fared thy grandsires, while thy beak was grow-
 ing—
 That suction-pipe, sheathing thy flexile knife?
Which bores my flesh, and sets my blood aflowing,
 Then pumps it up, to feed thy cursed life.
Once had they teeth, or mandibles, to gnaw,
 Which by disuse, may now have long been lost?
Or did they always bore, to feed their maw?
 Finding their tube and lance the smallest cost.
But if, by bit and bit, these grew complete,
 A shorter way they once must draw their food;
And, though they always needed drink and meat,
 Not always could they steal our lordly blood:
Or if, on us, thy race did always feed,
With budding lance, how could you make us bleed?

CXXII.

Thou'st proved, thou wretch, thy tool thou hast per-
        fected,
   To suit thy trade—to filch the blood of men;
Most fitly for thy trade thou art selected,
   And fitly crawls to life from stagnant fen.
What wast at first? blood-thirsty cunning thief!
   Who taught thee how, on other's blood to feed?
Could one so small, and in a life so brief,
   Learn how to make this earth's proud lord to bleed?
Or perhaps some grandsire, tasting blood by chance,
   Learnt, in our veins life's nectar he could find?
He having, somehow, gained that budding lance,
   Which now full grown, serves well thy knavish
        mind.
If oaths must damn us, thou art twice an evil—
A torment here, goading us to the devil.

CXXIII.

Still reading books 'tis scarcely wise to read,
   And seeking still what you so long have sought—
To follow dumbly to another's lead,
   And feed your mind on other thinker's thought.
Good books, at worst, may some new thoughts sug-
        gest;
   Bad books, at best, but serve all thought to scatter;

Minds nurtured by good books, their thought digest;
    Mind starves, though crammed, on bad books'
        worthless matter.
That book's a friend, that does a guide supply—
    Serve as a glass where nature is reflected;
But if not true, it turns my thought awry
    From that true course where thought should be
        directed.
Books show us what in nature we may find;
What do not so, do but mislead the mind.

CXXIV.

You leave the crowd, to muse in field and wood—
    Seek so to tune your soul to nature's voice,
The song of birds making your solitude,
    Then in your heart you look for nature's choice?
You would regard yourself as nature's tongue—
    Hope she through you some secret may reveal,
Or from your heart call forth some simple song,
    Answering the pressure of your soft appeal?
All things we meet, some secret have to show;
    If we but charm them with the proper spell,
They gladly tell us all that we may know,
    Reserving that they have no leave to tell:
When nature's open secrets we have read,
The heart still hungry, is by wondering fed.

CXXV.

Give me the truth, we often hear expressed:
    But do we always know the speaker's meaning?
We guess his wish, when we are so addressed,
    Not by his words, but by his special leaning.
I say, perchance, I think there is a God:
    The atheist thinks, the love of truth I'm mocking—
Or that all mind is in this thinking clod:
    The theist thinks my love of truth most shocking.
Perchance I doubt, to neither side inclined,
    But all of easy faith detest a skeptic;
Should I no merit in the question find,
    All sides agree I'm morally dyspeptic.
Give me the light, one in the dark might say—
Even love the night, if with the hope of day.

CXXVI.

Asking for truth, what is it that we ask ?
    Truth's but a word ; is knowledge what we want ?
To feed the mind is life's imperious task ;
    Our call for truth is oft but serious cant.
When partial views our coward minds enslave,
    With colored eye, tinting all mental light,
The truth we seek must flatter that we have ;
    What truth we love, must say we're in the right.

To bring the heart beneath stern truth's dominion—
    Let truth our pleasing prejudice subdue—
To change what truth condemns in old opinion,
    Are feats, our love of truth can seldom do :
Though fear of truth in others we contemn,
All truth but ours, as freely we condemn.

CXXVII.

To lies disguised in forms to please the mind,
    Though lies we ban, the heart still fondly clings ;
If lies gain welcome, when with truth combined,
    Truth oft is welcome for the lie it brings.
If truth, alone, can give vitality
    To what enduring lie would else decay ;
Then falsehood is but truth's mortality,
    And truth itself can never pass away.
In pleasing blindness, pleasing error dwells ;
    False eye sees truth where true no truth can see ;
While plausive lie a flattering story tells,
    Truth-seeing eye looks not where truth may be.
While lies keep power to give us pleasure,
Unwonted truth must wait a tardy leisure.

CXXVIII.

I live a slave, in bondage to the many,
    Working in silence, still without reward;
I meet with frowns, but not the smile of any;
    My work is scorned, or passed without regard.
Why then in ceaseless toil my life consume,
    Crowding with care a life of weary days?
What final shape can my reward assume,
    If kindred hearts my work may ne'er appraise?
This question, to my heart no tongue will answer;
    And still I work, though still unsatisfied;
From day to day some lingering hope I transfer
    That all meed will not ever be denied.
But such I find the terms on which I live,
That ill or well, this labour I must give.

CXXIX.

But wholesome thought still brings some satisfaction;
    Peace crowns the wish to leave the world my
        debtor;
Some pleasure ever comes from fruitful action,
    If by such action I the world may better.
Like pigmy suns, each centred in his sphere,
    We bend our fellow mortals in their course;

Loving or hating, giving joy or fear,
　'Mongst human atoms, each exerts a force.
I find each hour that what I hate repels;
　To what I love, I'm moved by soft desire;
Though what I loathe oft in my memory dwells,
　I would be only as I most admire:
Who would by living, then, the world improve,
Must be, in living, what the world can love.

CXXX.

Who is my judge? and how shall I be measured?
　Of worth, or worthless, is my life's effect?
Will this be banned? or by the future treasured,
　With time's addition, claiming time's respect?
If from myself my eye could stand aloof,
　Appraising justly what my soul gives forth,
And see as others might in my behoof,
　I might then know my labor's proper worth.
But so my labor I may never test;
　And so its value I may never know;
I might condemn what now I deem my best,
　If any best my labor has to show.
Life may in fruitless effort run to nought;
Yet partial judgment still must rule my thought.

CXXXI.

This man is rich; but I, he knows, am poor;
   Such wealth as his, 'tis sure must ne'er be mine;
I'm still repulsed from Fortune's guarded door;
   Still Fortune's sun disdains, on me to shine.
His lands are broad; no spot I call my own;
   His house is large ; I in cold sufferance sleep;
Earth groans to feed him; I a crust am thrown;
   I lack all things; he holds nature's treasure cheap:
He eyes my bareness with a scornful scowl,
   As if it did his pampered heart offend;
He bends his brows as if he thought my soul
   Should feel its fate must on his frown depend.
I pity his scorn, and scorn his poor opinion;
My soul lives not within his frown's dominion.

CXXXII.

Still in base toil I toil that I may live ;
   Unbottomed wants their hourly tribute ask ;
Still would I work, yet different work would give ;
   But others, not myself, dictate my task.
Heartwearying years my heart is barred all choice
   What labor I within these years might do ;
When I might in congenial work rejoice,
   Mere jin-horse-toil, Fate bids me then pursue.

My soul, my body's bidding must obey ;
   Hard Fate, despite my will, has willed it so ;
Its base regards hold me, from day to day,
   From that sweet toil with which my heart would
     go.
But nought it boots that still my heart rebels
Against a doom a kindless fate compels.

CXXXIII.

Youth's life we spend, to purchase means to live,
   And beggared youth is of youth's right bereft;
When life has charms, life's all we then must give,
   To feed what worthless remnant youth has left.
We fast, that we may with full pleasure feed;
   But fast until we lose all appetite ;
Then smothered joys, that youth alone can breed,
   We find will not return to breed delight.
What youth could love, youth must in youth forego,
   Content with hope youth's charm may still endure;
And when youth's passions still no longer glow,
   Youth's now dead hopes perchance we might
     secure.
Ah ! happy those who find this course reversed ;
Whose youth is not, with foodless hunger cursed.

CXXXIV.

What bliss might in true souls, by wealth, be
    wrought!
  Though woe to all who know but its abuse!
All own its need, yet 'tis too dearly bought,
  When bought by all for which we seek its use.
On tireless wing, through Summer's honeyed hours,
  By nature's guide, unerring instinct, led,
The provident bee despoils the nectared flowers
  Of sweets by which his winter life is fed:
As bees, so man, instinct, too, for his guide,
  Seeks wealth he tastes not in youth's hurrying
    strife;
His hopes of youth, in joys of age confide;
  He then despairs with youth's decaying life:
Unfed in youth, all nobler instincts die;
From frost of age, all youthful pleasures fly.

CXXXV.

Unblest by friends, I travel still through life:
  Though thronging crowds move on my daily
    course,
No voice I hear above the babbling strife,
  That touches love with sweet congenial force.
Thoughts roll on thoughts, and silently assume
  The forms deemed meet to stir congenial mind;

But dumbly must my thought, itself consume ;
  Nowhere my love and thought, their echo find.
O'er pregnant themes, my soul may inly brood—
  Its own inception, growth, and destiny—
Its ruling law—its instinct for the good—
  Its life in time, or in eternity :
Fraught with such thought, its voice may still be clear;
Its voice, still nowhere finds a kindred ear.

CXXXVI.

Here glowed with life, once dear familiar forms!
  But one by one, they with fleet hours have gone,
Swept from time's place, by time's unpitying storms,
  Leaving me here, to stranger hearts alone.
I, one lone tree, in ruined forest stand,
  Where blooming friends rejoiced once in their
      pride,
Waiting the axe, ringing in deadly hand,
  Knelling some doomed, stray, lingerer from my
      side.
Vanquished or victor in time's battling life,
  So different once, my heart now deems the same;
Those who smiled hope upon my entering strife,
  Now at its goal leave but a memoried name :
Hearts that with mine once beat in flattering trust,
In earth, again, have laid their wearied dust.

7

CXXXVII.

I stand alone in this wide universe,
   'Reft of all hearts youth's pleasures might en-
      hance—
Of all who could with youth's dead hopes converse,
   And share my then-that-was-to-be romance.
With fading time, hopes still retire from view,
   Yet few or none, to fill their place arise ;
And day by day life's hopes I must renew,
   Yet with new hopes, stay not old sympathies.
Now from old objects as my heart removes,
   And in new fields of gladness seeks to range,
It finds it must, alone, now change its loves :
   It changes not as other hearts would change.
Old friends are dead, though some are breathing still;
New friends come not, their empty place to fill.

CXXXVIII.

Ever in silence must I bear the load
   That lays such painful pressure on my heart ;
And, though despair strike deep his barbed goad,
   No friendly hand may soothe the festering smart.
Why was my heart ere made so sensitive,
   Finding such torture in such common ill?
The heart that in coarse strife is doomed to live
   Should have its sense obedient to its will.

My heart finds grief where others feel no pain;
　　Others find bliss where mine can find no joy;
What pains or pleasures o'er my heart obtain,
　　O'er other hearts, no kindred power employ.
Its craving is what my poor life denies;
It holds that cheap, which my poor life supplies.

CXXXIX.

Still looms the doubt that overclouds my soul,
　　Making its gloom a burden to my life,
Light making dark, and fairest day look foul,
　　Where peace should reign, still making direst
　　　　strife.
Yet smiles the sun, his smile, as ever bright,
　　Lighting my eye, but cheering not my heart;
And in his smile all living things delight;
　　Yet in their joy for me there is no part.
In present life my heart can find no rest,
　　Nor can it on the future's hope repose;
In life now past, deeming it knew its best,
　　A weary sameness, now, it only knows.
My future's hope, my past experience kills;
Though hope be dead, my fear sees future ills.

CXL.

The worm, whose world lies on some trembling leaf,
    The insect, reptile, bird, and servile beast—
All lives that nature gives, however brief,
    Their humblest owners make a life-long feast.
Their present joy they take without alloy;
    Their future life they see not in the past;
Remembered grief chills not their present joy;
    Their hearts are not with boding ills o'ercast.
Joy turns to grief, when I the future doubt;
    I need hope's light, to see a present bliss;
When present pleasures are to memory brought,
    All freshness I in their enjoyment miss.
For life's true joy, on hope I still must wait;
Hope's promise, still my memory will abate.

CXLI.

But wherefore should my heart its moaning keep,
    And gracious Fate a future boon intending?
Why groan awake, foul dreams dream in my sleep,
    While joy, not grief, is o'er my heart impending?
From veiled future, bodings undefined
    Threatened my heart in whisperings of some sad-
        ness;

But when the threat should be fulfilled, I find
    Not grief, but unexpected cause of gladness.
Does some good demon, near, but still unseen,
    Burthen my heart that ease may seem the lighter?
Give grief, that sense of joy may be more keen,
    As after eclipse, sun makes day seem brighter?
Poor heart! that can life's worth no better measure,
Than place a grief where stands a coming pleasure.

CXLII.

Foul fronted, hated, old, adversity!
    Fierce pain and fear, gaunt hunger and disease!
Dumb toil, disgrace, all-craving poverty!
    What may thy dateless enmity appease?
Offspring of passion, error, hankering sin,
    Of whirlwind, storm, insatiate fire and flood!
From reckless chance or vengeful crime begin
    Thy ills, that curse, alike, the vile and good.
Of other's sin, on me the fruit must fall;
    On me, another's crime must ruin bring;
Another's suffering must my heart appal,
    And malice wound it with its venomed sting.
Still may thy hate, perhaps, do the work of love,
If from my heart, some dross, thy fires remove.

CXLIII.

But as the winter, or death-frost in spring,
    Or foul distemper, riding on the wind,
Try with their deadly power, each living thing,
    Killing the weak, leaving the strong behind—
The whirlwind sweeps loose herbage from the field;
    Frost kills the fungus, born of summer breath ;
All summer's strength to winter's power must yield,
    Or buy its life, by braving powers of death:
So thou, stern god, may'st, perhaps, obscurely serve
    Some needful end, as does all wintry strife—
Curb vain excess—strain muscle, brain and nerve—
    By hunger's goad, spurring to nobler life.
We prosper now, by past adversity,
As fasting-present feeds futurity.

CXLIV.

Thou god of luck, that deem'st all merit cheap,
    Unseen in creatures of thy fond caprice,
Each good would'st thou, upon thy favorites heap—
    Gifts giving till thy giving grows to vice.
Thy petted few may take all thanklessly—
    Fume when self-measured wages are withheld—

Carp at their betters' havings, enviously :
    Still to their cravings dost thou fondly yield.
But we, base helots, missing thy regard,
    Doomed to base toil that life alone can measure,
Must with all thanks accept thy foul award,
    Begging base leave to serve thy fondling's pleasure.
Ah! hope to life, links with so sure a tie!
Or who would live, beneath thy rule to lie?

CXLV.

My body's powers now fail beneath their work;
    Not for sweet sleep's renewal do they pause;
Invading foes in their dominion lurk,
    And come in question of an ancient cause.
My pleasures, too, I find now drugged with pain;
    A lodged poison, I of old inherit;
O'er-mastering thoughts give action to the brain,
    And leave a taint still deeper on my spirit.
My nature's blest or baleful heritage
    Is ever potent in my good or ill;
Good would I foster, and my ill assuage,
    But changeless past, its mission must fulfil.
Heaven's friend, that man we may most rightly deem,
Who kills past poison in life's present stream.

CXLVI.

I saw, to-day, a man without a home:
  No wonder, then, he was without a friend;
To feed life's want, a beggar he must roam;
  Yet shrunk he fiercely from his nearing end.
His health was sore, and he had lost a limb;
  His clothes were thin, and with the cold he shook;
His hair was white; his sight was growing dim;
  He looked his case; alas! how sad a look.
With age and want, and with his body maimed,
  No home, no friend, no health, and nearly blind—
With all the ills by Fortune's malice framed,
  He still in living, pleasure hoped to find.
The world's best gifts, some deem too poor a guer-
      don;
He stript of all, still deemed not life a burden.

CXLVII.

A king discrowned—bereft of regal might,
  Breathing no longer honor-breathing breath,
Ruling men's wills no more, by sovereign right,
  Though still he lives, life deems he living death:
A merchant, falling from his haughty state
  To that his clerk contentedly could fill,

Now men no longer on his pleasure wait,
　To him all worth of future life is killed.
The king is poor, though in the merchant's place;
　The merchant groans where once his clerk could
　　smile;
The beggared clerk, hungering in poor disgrace,
　Now justly does his abject fate revile:
'Tis good or ill as we look up or down;
Want craves a crust, a king demands a crown.

CXLVIII.

But how shall I my craving soul appease?
　Where find the food its want to satisfy? ,
Can dumb, unacted thought, its torture ease?
　Or thought in deeds, its hunger gratify?
To meet the hourly call of clamorous life—
　Do vulgar duty for some sordid end—
Leaves still unsoothed that fretful, eager strife
　That does not on life's petty ills depend.
Dumb passions, dying daily in my breast—
　Imagined deeds that on the mind intrude—
The crowding thoughts that throng to be expressed—
　But keener make the want they should preclude.
To quench the pain its hungry fire imparts,
My heart must lend its fire to kindred hearts.

CXLIX.

We say man's life is imaged by the seasons,
  Summer, autumn, winter, led by hopeful spring;
But how few hearts hold memory's imaged reasons
  To deem all seasons do their fruitage bring.
We find, indeed, the spring with promise bright,
  And find, indeed, spring's promise often blasted—
Find sunless summers missing, in their flight,
  Those summer fruits, hope had in spring fore-
    tasted :
And tranquil pleasures, autumn should possess,
  Where hope of spring and summer fruits should
    centre,
Are swallowed in a wintry wilderness,
  While life itself goes out in early winter.
With hopeful aims, man's earlier hours are rife.
In hopeless gloom, man creeps through later life.

CL.

Man's life is but a day unwisely spent;
  He aims at bliss that he would reap from folly;
Late wisdom, early folly may repent,
  Though yields he still, his fate to blindness wholly.
With eager heart, life's journey he pursues,
  A treacherous fancy ever for his guide ;

What fruit he finds, his appetites abuse :
　　They please a moment, then are cast aside.
But joys that pleased, he finds please not again,
　　And new ones grow not, as his journey grows;
Seeking now novel joys, he seeks in vain,
　　But finds old joys may now bring novel woes.
Were this, life's all, how vain were life indeed—
If age find misery, life's sole earthly meed.

CLI.

But when I stand upon the river's brink,
　　Watching its turbid body as its flows,
I contemplate its origin, and think
　　How like a human soul its body grows.
The streams it gathers in its wandering course,
　　Gather in turn, the various streams they find ;
Each rill is various from its various source ;
　　So is the stream, of various streams combined :
So does man's life, from various sources grow ;
　　Each day gives what no other day can give ;
So does man's life its various substance show,
　　Past life deciding how to-day I live :
Foul life, to-day, makes life to-morrow, foul ;
Foul streams of life must still pollute the soul.

CLII.

Whence flow the richest streams of human life?
  Whence does the soul its dearest tribute gain?
Life, from the heart, when purified by strife,
  Its richest treasure, ever must obtain.
And yet the heart does but the ore supply,
  Mere earthy dross, till tempered in the mind;
Not on crude passion must true life rely,
  But passion which cold reason has refined.
Wild passion's but a flame in maniac hands;
  What might be bliss, its recklessness destroys;
But passion where sure reason's law commands,
  Is nature's fount of life's perennial joys.
To nature's will, the willing heart must bow;
Then through the heart, will nature's music flow.

CLIII.

The lark, day's herald, on aspiring wing,
  My spirit calls once more from mimic death,
Heaven's smile rewaking joy in every thing,
  While feathered throats give thanks in hurrying
      breath.
Would we but nature's gentle wish obey,
  And cloth our life, from sun to sun, with pleasure,

What need we but this perfect summer day,
    Trees, birds and flowers, sweet health and leisure?
But vainly nature's sweetest angels strive
    To touch our hearts from sun or bird or flower,
While those fierce passions in our bosom live
    That live to strive for baleful wealth and power:
For basest appetites, we fiercely carve,
While life's best wants, we basely leave to starve.

CLIV.

But on we go, still following through the world
    Some beckoning pleasure we in vain would clasp;
Or, tasting, from our lips the cup is hurled,
    To leave, for fruit, but ashes in our grasp.
We try those pleasures sense and passion give,
    Which gleam a moment in their lurid fire;
Proving what joys in love and friendship live,
    We prove how oft hope mocks our fond desire.
Where does enduring pleasure then abide?
    Such as the past, such will the future have?
Or must we still pursue our mocking guide,
    Expecting joys, such as the past ne'er gave?
Those memoried pleasures seen in retrospect,
In falling years, we may no more expect.

CLV.

But, " Light that led astray was light from Heaven?"
   If this was so, I know not when 'twas so :
If wrong we go when Heavenly light is given,
   When hell shall blind us, then how shall we go?
By passion's light, not Heaven's, we are misled,
   And pride-led oft, when we seem conscience-
      moved ;
Wrong acts, on which no ray from Heaven is shed,
   Of Heavenly birth are deemed because they're
      loved.
We think aright oft when we act awrong,
   And wrongly think oft when we act aright ;
To mind nor heart, alone, our acts belong;
   If heart give fire, from mind should come the light.
By heavenly light, no soul can miss its way ;
'Tis passion, blind, that leads the soul astray.

CLVI.

You see the cloud yon, hanging on the sky?
   In seeming bulk not larger than a crow?
Observe awhile, and you may, by and by,
   See momently, its dark dimensions grow :
Within, or near, some power there does obtain
   To draw new matter from surrounding space ;

With bulk it does some fiery spirit drain
    That rules with ruthless force each neighboring
        place.
This man, we here in history contemplate
    As strewing weal and woe along his course,
Grew to his present, from so low a state,
    By gathering substance from each neighboring
        source.
The cloud, indeed, a mindless power displays;
But he, a mind 'gainst heaven itself arrays.

CLVII.

The boom of guns, again rolls on the air!
    Once more proclaiming direful victory;
More havoc, still, is done, beyond repair—
    More deeds to stain the page of history—
More blood of foe, by friend or brother shed,—
    More lives of friends, by friends are cut away;
More hearts must bleed, with those that erst have
        bled,
    Or seethe in hatred, time can ne'er allay.
Relentless lust of empire still must rage;
    In freedom's name, self-rule must be destroyed;
To right a wrong, wrong war must work his rage,
    And in God's name, wrong war be justified.
Those equal rights men oft so fiercely claim,
They now as fiercely crush, in freedom's name.

CLVIII.

Accursed war again roars, self is right;
  Self answering roars, all self, but self, is wrong;
And paltering conscience trims her blear-eyed sight,
  To find all rights, to conquering might belong.
Destruction laughs; gaunt Famine sweeps his rear,
  Havoc, uncurbed, taking all hideous forms;
Hell reigns on earth, till, terror conquering fear,
  Black death grows fair, and now no more alarms.
Self's rightful claims, self rightly may disown;
  Self doubts fair acts may hide some foul intent;
Be then no heed to self's self-favoring shown,
  Self claims, to self, Heaven's 'venging power is
    lent.
" Vengeance is mine," once breathed from Heavenly
    dust;
Small faith has self, Heaven's patient power is just.

CLIX.

But war is o'er, and now you count the cost;
  In counting cost, may you not count yours gains?
Though victory, of glorious victory you boast,
  The better fruit, your beaten foe retains.
But peace—again hosannas welcome peace,
  From tongues that pæans sung for vengeful war;

And now destruction's reddened hand must cease,
  His hand, still red, his havoc would repair.
Not so the tiger, in his angry mood;
  He's doomed to kill, or doomed himself to die;
Though war we not on human foes for food,
  With tiger's hate, we human foes destroy.
How long shall it continue nature's plan,
That tiger's law shall guard the rights of man.

CLX.

All-mastering sun ! that lend'st thy fire and light,
  To fit this earth for man's first breathing place;
Since man came forth from blank, eternal night,
  What changes hast thou seen come o'er his race !
Thou saw'st man ere he might be called man—
  Alas ! how often may'st thou do so still—
While still enfolded in some foreformed plan,
  Which he, by upward striving, might fulfil.
Thou'st seen—what sin-spawned suffering hast thou
      seen !
  To-day, what well earned suffering may'st thou
      see !
Still passion rules, as if no pain had been ;
  Still reason scarce asserts her right to be:
Thou saw'st man come—wilt look on when he goes,
But not when cease, man's self-inflicted woes.

8

CLXI.

But when, ah! when will that late day appear,
    When Truth shall rule where Error ruled so long,
And Right have might to stay dissembling Fear,
    And kill the brood of foul prolific Wrong!
When will truth-nurtured Might have power to chain
    That lust-born thing, still fed with earth and gore,
And fix on earth his heaven-appointed reign,
    And bid man lie for crouching Fear no more!
When will man see in his most sacred claim,
    A sacred duty, sacredly respected;
When will man's heart seek as its sovereign aim,
    A bliss, in bliss from other hearts reflected!—
Then will man's struggling pain be surely earning
That hour, for which, man's soul is hourly yearning.

CLXII.

Changed were the world, were self's whole action just;
    Were selfish hearts, on sacred honor set;
Could all hearts wisely selfish honor trust—
    In other's due, could self its claim forget;
Could self its own, see in another's right,
    True good discerning from the seeming true,

Finding, or seeking, nowhere self-delight,
  While unself be defrauded of its due:
Could self but nature's changeless purpose see,
  And nowhere read her changeless will amiss,—
Did self discern her sovereign will to be,
  Till right be done, self knows no sovereign bliss:
Were self such self, changed were the world indeed!
But ere such change, self-love must change his creed.

CLXIII.

Yon truant wife, her wedded home has fled—
  Her sin-struck home, now worse than death-
    bereaved;
This one, so true! pines on a death-struck bed,
  Condemned past hope, if for few hours reprieved;
That greening mound conceals a murderer's prey,
  Murdered to glut the murderer's maw with food;
Yon stands the gibbet, glooming summer's day,
  Preaching to heedless hearers, blood for blood.
Gross surfeit palls; want curses hunger's goad;
  Self, self destroys, that self alone would save,
Or sinks, bearing a self-imposed load,
  Through virtuous sin, seeking a self-made grave:
Vice runs with vice, till vice outruns disgrace;
Virtue 'gainst vice, still runs a losing race.

CLXIV.

We meet again, across those stormful years
    That show Time's office in this sea of life;
The puling child, now lordly man appears;
    The haughty youth, a trembling wreck of strife.
Still, seem these years but as a hurrying dream,
    Linking blank past with blank futurity?
Yet life itself is but a conscious gleam
    That flashes from a dark eternity.
We're each to-day, still looking for to-morrow;
    To-morrow brings not what to-day expected;
And though each day we sound a deeper sorrow,
    To each new day our hearts are hope-directed:
Something unfound we seek, from stage to stage;
Even summer flowers, seek in fierce winter's rage.

CLXV.

We, on the stream of time, mere bubbles, float,
    Instinct a moment with a conscious life,
And but some passing gleams and shadows note,
    Of joy and grief that cross our course of strife.
Our place in time, and hours of joy or pain,
    Seem but the sport of ever varying forces;

Our thought and will, the objects we would gain,
  Are ever changing with life's changing sources.
Knowing not how to-morrow we may be—
  Whether in joy or grief—in love or hate—
Or if ere then, life's ending we may see—
  In helpless trust, we're drifting on our fate.
Though on to-day, to-morrow's life is pending,
We live as if, to-day, all life was ending.

CLXVI.

This bubble life, seeming all chance directed,
  Comes and returns, obedient to its cause;
Its cause with cause, through time must be con-
      nected,
  And man, through time, moves on a stream of laws.
We see not whence this stream of causes springs;
  Its source is lost within the viewless past;
We see each hour some new effect it brings,
  But time-bound vision sees no first or last.
That stream of power that ends in forming man,
  Flows ever from that unconceived abyss,
Where fate or purpose framed the primal plan
  Of all that was, will be, and all that is.
I stop and ask, with wonder ever new,
How man and nature, into being grew.

CLXVII.

What is that power, which seizing lifeless earth—
 Mere units, differing as their motions differ—
Through ages struggling, brings that soul to birth,
 Which here, in time, begins to know and suffer?—
Tempering base clay through cyclonean storms
 Of torrid heat, and zones of wintry strife—
Casting, recasting, mind through lowliest forms,
 From stage to stage, to terms of nobler life—
Then in that gathering sea of life in death,
 Maturing stores to fill that mastering plan
That strains a thinking fire from dust and breath—
 A life for Heaven, perhaps, starting here in man?
May mind, yet, in some mindless substance find
Some mindless power with power to form a mind?

CLXVIII.

You see no mystery, round your earthly home?—
 None that mere changing force may not explain;
Dead force framing live souls that go and come,
 And, spring and offspring, but an hour remain.
A viewless speck, viewless to naked sight,
 Conceals an all-sufficient power to be

Formed forth a moss or oak, a man or mite,
    But which, you own no prescient power to see.
This mindless power, working in mindless earth,
    Sends forth, and clothes with form, a conscious
        spirit;
And soul from soul, thus from the dust has birth,
    By soul projecting power, each does inherit.
This change you see, that issues forth in mind,
But see no plan, hiding a thought behind.

CLXIX.

My eye, mere moving ether turns to light;
    My touch, some kindred motion turns to heat;
From moving air, my ear invents delight;
    From motion, too, my tongue makes sour and
        sweet:
The radiant hues that paint the falling shower,
    The blending tones that charm my trembling ear,
The scent that greets me from the opening flower,
    Are not without, as they without appear.
My senses are soul-catering instruments,
    And by their action, on the world I feed;
My soul, through them, that wondrous show invents,
    That solely serves my soul's perpetual needs:
Though inward are, what shows appear without,
That they are outward, none have power to doubt.

CLXX.

From foul, rank earth, June roses draw perfume;
   From honeyed roses, hornets venom draw;
Fruits melt to song, that singing birds consume,
   And leaves to silk, that painted spinners gnaw.
The corn and poppy drain the self same earth,
   One feeding life, one hiding treacherous death;
Our pains and pleasures have a kindred birth:
   What gives a blessing may a curse bequeath.
To conquering life, dissolves the lifeless clod:
   From earth-fed blood, does life that substance
      drain,
That turns to thought of brute or demi-god,
   By life's transmuting power within the brain.
Life-tempered dust kissed by the wandering wind,
Then courses forth the time's self-questioning mind.

CLXXI.

'Mong outward things, my eye discerns a duty,
   Or duty o'er them, from my eye is thrown;
From outward things my eye receives a beauty,
   Or outward things give back my eye its own.
A pain seen outward, gives me inward pity;
   Another's moan will fill my eye with tears;

That which my eye sees as grotesque and witty,
    To witless eyes, a thing of course appears.
Some mystic power, that in man's spirit lies,
    Creates that spirit which his spirit quaffs;
The grosser world, his grosser need supplies;
    That world he makes, in which he weeps and
        laughs.
How may this godlike wonder, then, be stated?
Is man's best world, by man himself created?

CLXXII.

You see the thing now hurled across the distance,
    Giving the rock-ribbed earth this trembling jar,
Its force—such mockery of man's poor resistance—
    The breath of nature's fierce intestine war.
Imprisoned sunbeams, from yon burning light,
    Long ages buried in cold, lightless earth,
Awakened in their concentrated might,
    Now from their prison, yon are rushing forth;
And that wild contest, fire with water wages,
    Which no created hand could e'er subdue,
Man's mind controls where yon it fiercely rages,
    And bends its force to ends he would pursue.
You thundering mass, whose flight outspeeds the
        wind,
Flies screaming triumph to man's conquering mind.

CLXXIII.

Yon ship, that seems now hanging in the clouds,
　Or as 'twere mirrowed in this sea of glass,
Obeys the speck yon moving in the shrouds,
　As if his soul informed its mindless mass.
The wind may rage, and hourly change his course,
　And bend his might to make yon frame a wreck;
Man's feeble arm still guides his ruthless force,
　And holds his wild and ruffian power in check.
The wind may rage, the ocean roar and swell,
　As if they viewed man's daring will with scorn;
Man still defies the power he could not quell,
　And by their fury, on his course is borne.
Though from their rage, man often meets disaster;
He by his wit, their masterly power can master.

CLXXIV.

We meet appalled, the lightning's blinding flash,
　That strikes or spares ere we can think of care;
In crouching dread, we 'wait the thunder's crash,
　That comes now crushing through the rifted air.
The flaming mass, by which the air is rent,
　That strews destruction o'er its fiery way,

Is by man's wit, on peaceful missions sent:
    Its flash now fixed, turns darkest night to day.
In patient work, its might obeys man's will,—
    Conveys man's thought, or man, from place to
        place,—
Builds up, tears down, and shames the artist's skill—
    Kills time, and turns to nought the widest space:
The ruthless flame that from the heavens is hurled,
Will write man's thought, and flash it round the
        world.

CLXXV.

Still from his bed, yon mighty River falls!
    And still his fall, the trembling earth confounds!
His 'wildered terror, still the heart appals;
    His endless, boundless roar, the brain astounds.
Above his huge, upheaving, struggling breast,
    In foaming clouds his breath forever lies,
And radiant bows, see! on his bosom rest!
    And with all hues, stain moonlight as it flies.
Resounding through his countless ages past,
    His one-toned anthem swells on fancy's ear;
And while sweet awe is o'er all feeling cast,
    I in his presence, still rejoice and fear:
No feeling but of him, my heart retains;
His music, o'er all sound and silence reigns.

CLXXVI.

Yon sovereign orb pours down a sovereign force,
　　Which in my soul-ruled eye is turned to light;
And there those hues of beauty have their source,
　　Which move my spirit with such pleasing might—
Those grateful sounds that make my spirit thrill,
　　Or grating noise that makes my body shiver,
To being spring forth from that sensuous skill
　　That changes feeling with air's changing quiver—
In me, by motion of that vital earth,
　　Which formed me, or is framed itself by me,
Brought forth from death, those living thoughts have
　　　　birth,
　　Which through my spirit, gain their power to be:
A mystic force, I into space can cast,
To bring forth life and love from desert waste.

CLXXVII.

All things of sense, sense brings to store the mind,
　　By sense are formed, or say, by sense revealed;
The rainbow shines not when the eye is blind;
　　And from deaf ears, all music is concealed.
The air we breathe, the solid ground we tread,
　　The varying light by which the world is shown,
The thunder cloud that bursts above my head,
　　Till known to sense, are not to reason known.

No reasoning could divine those wondrous shapes
  That are each hour by fruitful life renewed;
And life itself, both sense and thought escapes,
  Though life is with both sense and thought endued.
Whence thought may be, thought may most fitly
    ponder;
But thought will still be thought's enduring wonder.

CLXXVIII.

This figured earth must mingle with the dust—
  No vestige of its life-fed form remain;
But may I nurse the still abiding trust,
  Its soul claims not enduring life in vain?
Its life's a stream, feeding a standing lake;
  Or wasting fuel, serving constant flame;
Unresting atoms do this figure make,
  Which ever seems, but never is the same.
But as this change still feeds a growing spirit,
  And spirit builds from body's fleet decay,
Some sentient substance, may this soul inherit,
  That with this body may not turn to clay.
But could man's reasoning prove this reasoning so,
Then, for itself, might reasoning, reason show.

CLXXIX.

Still does the mystery wait for man to solve,
  Braving the present as it braved the past;
Sad, pondering minds, the mystery still revolve,
  Yet o'er its night, no ray of light have cast.
Do I exist?   What fool am I to ask?
  It seems I do; on seems I may not rest;
I reason call; but she declines the task;
  She's dumb, except when seeming does suggest.
Yet, will the stubborn query still persist,
  With how, or why, or whence, this seeming show?
I know that I and all things do exist;
  Anon 'tis whispered, I but seem to know:
From all that sense and reason then can give,
In sense and reason, I but seem to live.

CLXXX.

The sun has turned away his burning face,
  Leaving us wandering darkly in the night;
His sister sits not in her heavenly place,
  And nature mourns her sweet and saddening light.
But in yon dome that bounds my wondering gaze,
  Are clouds of suns firing the heavenly main;
Their numbers, all mind's feeble powers amaze,
  Thinking their vastness stuns the struggling brain.

Their rays, which strike the eye with twinkling light,
   That through long ages past were on the wing,
Tell not what now is in the home of night;
   Of time, as place, remote they tidings bring:
But are there suns where suns there seem to be?
Or are there not, but only seem to be?

CLXXXI.

What is being?   Then, what can seeming be?
   We seeming see, but how is being shown?
We seeming know, because we seeming see,
   But can what is, be by this seeming known?
That being is, from seeming we conclude;
   But what seems not, the mind can never know;
All things that seem not, then, the mind elude,
   And for the real, we must take the show.
Beneath this show is something more concealed?
   When senses sleep, are worlds no longer here?
How can the truth to us ere be revealed?
   All sense is dumb, nor reason can we hear.
But still we seek what we can never know;
We being seek, but merely find the show.

CLXXXII.

But with this show, shall mind be satisfied,
    Craving no more the something under show?—
Or craving still, its craving still denied,
    Still wonder if true being it may know?
Sense seizes matter; matter reason flies;
    Matter dwells in space, of space what can we find?
Changes pass in time; what's time then reason
        cries?
    Thus matter, time, and space, elude the mind.
Must reason ask how matter is composed?
    What attributes, blank time and space possess?
Must reason seek what ne'er may be supposed?
    Its impotence, must reason ne'er confess?
The universe dissolves in glowing thought;
And thought itself, in thinking, comes to nought.

CLXXXIII.

Then must I question still, great nature's source,
    Though nothing of her source I e'er may know?
May I not rest in viewing nature's course,
    But must still ask whence nature's changes flow?
She shows her power in every form I meet—
    Yon in the worlds glowing in distant space,
Here in the flower now smiling at my feet,
    With wondering eye, her protean power I trace.

But still from me, her secret she conceals;
  My why, or whence, or wherefore, she denies;
Of plan or purpose, she no more reveals,
  Than what within my dark experience lies.
But silence does not give my passion rest;
Her silence gives her mystery double zest.

CLXXXIV.

What is man's final station here on earth?
  Is he the full-grown fruit of nature's past?
Or does she promise by his earthly birth,
  Though latest born, he yet is not the last?
She's rich in means, and ever holds them cheap;
  Leaving one favorite, thousands pass away;
Sowing profusely, she will sparsely reap;
  But what she seals, she holds above decay.
Making mankind, she would perfect the man;
  The man, in turn, she makes her instrument;
His aim she bends to aid her future plan,
  And serving her, he finds his sole content.
Still man's best efforts blindly seek their mark;
They seek her end, but seek it in the dark.

  9

CLXXXV.

Did there in time a purpose once exist
    That man should be, and therefore is man here?—
A will, moving the power that does persist
    In forming man—guiding his blind career?
From purpose, if this stream of changes flows,
    Still bringing thence no tidings of its source,
Where shall it end? if end we may suppose:
    But end nor source, we see of nature's course.
Man springs from earth—again returns to earth;
    Worlds do, 'tis said, from thinnest vapor spring—
In vapor end, to find a second birth:
    Thus nature moves in one eternal ring.
Unpurposed this, what mind can e'er believe!
Its purpose, yet, what mind can e'er conceive!

CLXXXVI.

All life, it seems, begins in protoplasm;
    The chick is but albuman in the shell;
But here does nature bridge her deepest chasm,
    And hide that secret which she hides so well.
This substance, too, that bears this novel name,
    Being itself life's substance and its cause,
By complex and more complex mixture came,
    As atoms wed and wed by chemic laws.

Here looms, again, our scientific notion,
    That mind is but transformed material force;
And as all force is but atomic motion,
    Thought grows as atoms do each other course.
We eat, or die: why argument, then, bandy?
We know all Nature's modus operandi.

CLXXXVII.

On this dead ball, I hang in barren space,
    In thought and substance, bound to parent earth;
And this you deem my final resting place,
    My being claimed by that which gave it birth.
But had earth power to will that I should be?
    Or, without will, yet soul producing force?
Or must I deem these atoms forming me,
    Derive their thinking from the thunder's source?
Is thought inherent in the ground I tread?
    Or in the viewless air that gives me breath?
Or from that sun by which the world is fed,
    Is that derived which drew this life from death?
Or can earth, air, and yon sun's fire, combined,
From thoughtless matter, bring forth thoughtful
      mind?

CLXXXVIII.

We'll think yon cloud that o'er the sun now passes,
   That winds may turn and tumble as they list,
Is then a congeries of human gasses,
   Not as it seems, a mass of fleecy mist.
In fancy's eye, too, let it take that figure
   Which human atoms take on here below,
Their motion driving off death's freezing rigour,
   Motion transmuted, giving power to know.
These atoms, then, their motion so control,
   And in their mass such changes shall be wrought,
That those interior shall be turned to soul,
   And those without shall all be ruled by thought.
Souls formed of cloud, we'd deem a wond'rous birth;
A thing of course, we deem them formed of earth.

CLXXXIX.

Still, mindless force built up this sentient frame,
   Which, by and by, became mind's instrument,
To turn dead matter into conscious flame,
   Or drain mind-substance from dead forces spent:
Then looks the soul forth from its dwelling place—
   This house it built, as thunder builds the cloud—
Bids shows of beauty glow in lightless space—
   Bids music from dead silence speak aloud.

Birds sing but as my soul is musical;
　　'Tis coloring eye that paints their plumage bright;
Mind makes its thought from gross material—
　　From silent darkness, calls forth sound and light.
How glibly may these sounding words be said;
How faint the light they on life's mystery shed.

CXC.

So did this soul, which knows the universe,
　　Live as mere vapour in that primal mist,
Whose primal power, its substance did disperse
　　Through that great whole whose part it did exist;
And that which judges, now, of right and wrong,
　　Was, then, but moving atoms spread through
　　　　space;
And those that now I deem to me belong,
　　Some chance has brought to fill this conscious
　　　　place.
I am, in soul as body, then, a part
　　Of atoms which some force through space did
　　　　scatter,
And which, from death to life one moment start;
　　The next go forth again as lifeless matter;
Such change, it seems, to matter is assigned,
That mud to-day, to-morrow may be mind.

CXCI.

And then this particle that says, I know,
    And gives the universe a sensuous being,
Though spirit called, is but atomic flow—
    Mere pigmy balls, before each other fleeing.
'Tis so, you think, or else how can it be?
    Is not this body fed with lifeless matter?
If not so fed, then dies life's energy,
    And with the body, must the spirit scatter.
These atoms, perhaps, say, "Let us change to
        thought;"
    Or, perhaps, their little neighbors bid them think;
Perhaps mind is thus from mindless matter brought,
    Then mind may, perhaps, to mindless matter sink:
I then, perhaps, see through nature's deep disguise;
And ignorant once, your words, perhaps, make me
        wise.

CXCII.

This soul, that gives the world its bad and good—
    This dear unknown that speaks of I and me—
All thought and mind are mere transmuted mud,
    Which in its change, gains power to hear and see.
The stuff, then, too, here changed to ruling thought,
    Was atoms, not as now, at neighboring distance;
But from far regions were together brought,
    Their union bringing sense of their existence.

Or was each atom, then, a conscious elf,
    Each seeking each, to form this soul communion?
Or, as you think, this thing I call myself
    Was mindless stuff, ere meeting in this union?
Blind atoms, then, by wandering chance combined,
From distant realms have come, to form this mind.

CXCIII.

And chance, wise chance! conferred this soul on me—
    Me on myself, by chance-constructed law;
No mind, you're sure, decreed that I should be;
    From mindless force, wise chance this mind could
        draw.
God slept till I, through chance, obtained my being;
    If waking now, his waking had no choice;
God saw his work first through my power of seeing;
    Heaven heard no music till I tuned my voice.
In me, you think, God first possessed a mind?
    If I should dose, God's mind would then grow dull;
But when my soul puts forth its powers combined,
    Then, as God's soul, I am most worshipful.
I dreamt not, though I deemed myself a wonder,
God learnt through me, how wisely he could blunder.

CXCIV.

All force with force, we say, is correlated—
   That heat and light are but converted motion;
But when this force, in terms of sense is stated,
   Then force, 'twould seem, is changed into a notion.
A motion's but a body changing places,
   If not on curves, on lines that then are straight—
That onward moves, or, perhaps, its course retraces,
   And by mere speed, perhaps, forming light and
      heat.
But by and by, such motion finds the brain,
   In contact there, with other motion brought;
As motions still, these motions must remain,
   Or by their contact, are they changed to thought?
Granted; but then what reason can we find,
That motion in the brain should turn to mind?

CXCV.

But pardon me for speaking of the mind;
   The thing, I own, is now quite out of fashion;
We've consciousness, in various modes combined,
   But not a thing producing thought and passion:
We've streaming thought, each single thought a
      ripple,
   Each, as they pass, saying, I feel and know;
And then, if nought this course of motion cripple,
   They through their channels pass with even flow:

They pass, and do not tarry in the brain,
  But give their place to those that may succeed;
And strange, these ripples will return again,
  When 'I' some portion of them chance to need.
But 'I' is fixed, and bids the past return?
Of that, this 'I' would something gladly learn.

CXCVI.

In sounding words, we may be wondrous wise;
  And sounding words, perhaps, do the work of
      things;
Then, hunting thought's a bootless enterprise,
  Where words bring that content which meaning
      brings.
Why should we ask with such unbending rigor,
  That words shall always be the signs of thought?
When thoughts will come not, why not take a figure,
  By which some obvious thing to mind is brought?
We'll figure mind, then, as a river flowing,
  Continuous thought, the river's constant flow;
Though streams show not how mind has power of
      knowing,
  We've streaming mind, minus the power to know.
Pray, let's seem wise, if only wise in words;
Much wordy wisdom, can our guides afford.

CXCVII.

We something know, and much from inference
    draw,
  Of nature's method, and of nature's work;
She hides her purpose, but reveals her law,
  By which we climb to where some secrets lurk.
We know, for instance, matter seeks a centre—
  That worlds on centres some times do revolve;
Here one of nature's secrets do we enter—
  How suns and satelites, she might evolve.
But worlds, we think, grow dense and ever denser;
  So must their substance once be very thin;
With pressure, heat grows still and still intenser,
  Then in cold vapor, perhaps, did worlds begin:
As clocks run down, worlds seek a falling plain;
But being down, who winds them up again?

CXCVIII.

Once on a time, as story books begin,
  This universe was into mist resolved;
Which on its centre then was forced to spin:
  Hence were all worlds and living things evolved.
We must infer, then, by all laws mechanic,
  This mist must break up into divers rings;
And though, at first, their motions were Titanic,
  Their law would cut its way to smaller things—

To worlds like this—of varying range, in fine,
    This whirling mist, in time, was sure to come,
Some dark, while some with native light would
        shine,
    And by some tie, at birth forbid to roam.
But still we seek that power that formed the mist—
And still the power that did that power resist.

CXCIX.

But mass with mass will surely aggregate,
    As sure as atom will to atom draw;
And mass from mass, perhaps, too, will segregate,
    If we may keep our faith in nature's law.
The force now locked within this whirling mass,
    Is still the force that held it in division;
And into mist this world again would pass,
    Should but its equal meet it in collision.
How need we, then, an adventitious force,
    To melt a world again to thinnest air?
This universe, stopt whirling in its course,
    Would to its pristine form again repair:
This world so stopt, were sure a changed thing;
But whence the world, to countermarch its ring?

CC.

As nature was, still must she ever be ?
　No change, by mortal mind may be supposed;
No course but hers, can human fancy see ;
　And faith, compelled, in her must be reposed.
The light that surges o'er the field of day,
　The force that moves this world along its course,
The heat that turns the winter's blast away,
　Do all grow weaker as they leave their source.
The stream and streamlet make the swelling river;
　Cause brings effect, effect must follow cause ;
While pound still weighs a pound, as it must ever,
　So men and worlds must yield to changeless laws.
But man, an insect in a water drop,
Sees but a point; there does his vision stop.

CCI.

Standing here on this point in boundless space,
　All things around excluding from my thought,
Whence can I, then, my sole existence trace;
　Or how was I into existence brought?
I blend my being with all things around,
　Or add it to an ever lengthening chain,
Then ask how all things their existence found?
　An echo only, does my question gain.

Was there a time when nothing did exist?
  In time, from nothing, did existence grow?
Did that of all being does consist,
  No birth into existence ever know?
In reverent awe, my trembling soul is dumb,
To endless silence, must my soul succumb.

CCII.

I am; what other wonder may be stated,
  Though I all seeming wonders should rehearse?
These gorgeous shows, my spirit has created,
  And hung as raiment round the universe.
I am; and therefore does the world exist;
  It takes all hue and beauty from my seeing;
These glowing forms that do in space persist,
  Have in my spirits act, alone, their being.
These shows, then, which my spirit has compounded,
  As ruling powers now do my spirit enter;
And in their realm my spirit is impounded,
  Though all their power does in my spirit centre:
No wonder lives within this wondrous show,
That lives not in my wondrous power to know.

CCIII.

O wondrous soul, where all things mirrored lie,
    That firmly sets bright worlds in outward state,
Then nimbly changing, deems an inward eye
    All outward visions solely does create—
And inwardly, as outward, all things measures,
    Making them bear an outward ill or good,
From things indifferent, framing pain and pleasures,
    Deeming unjust, what contravenes its mood—
Self-built, or built up by some mystic force,
    Which centred in thy mystic self must dwell,
Drawing soul-substance from a soulless source,
    Thou fram'st in time a place of ill or well.
But were thy being's force all centred in thy will,
Then might thyself decree thy good or ill.

CCIV.

Decree, dear soul, what thou hast scope to be,
    In realms that own thy will as sovereign power;
Though all thou wouldst, thy power may not decree,
    What now thou will'st, may bless some unlived
        hour.
Thy being now, with past shall future link,
    And breathe forth life that still returns again;
What good or ill thou now shalt act or think,
    Thy good or ill forever shall remain:

A discord now, a discord must be still;
  This moment's music ever must be sweet;
A strife now quelled by thy triumphant will,
  A strife the less thy future has to meet.
While thou art sovereign of thy sovereign mood,
Thou still art sovereign of thy sovereign good.

CCV.

Again farewell to one more year now fled,
  Leaving its blest or baleful fruit with me;
Life's task is now one year the nearer sped;
  One year's more change now was, that was to be.
Farewell, thou past—thou mighty thing that was—
  Dead nothing—parent of the living now—
Gulph of each present—fount of all to pass—
  Thou now dead sea, whence all life's waters flow.
Thou'rt gone forever, yet thou rul'st me still;
  Though nursed by thee, from thee I ever fly;
Each moment I some end of thine fulfill—
  Each moment end what still may never die.
Flying, I still stand on thy brinkless shore,
From deep behind, rushing on deep before.

MOTHER MONKFORD'S MEETING,

AND OTHER POEMS.

MOTHER MONKFORD'S MEETING.

The heavens are black: where stars should be,
Earth's fire-rent pall, alone, I see!
The rain roars down! the lightnings flash!
While through the din, the thunders crash!
And still the winds are gathering might,
To throw new terrors o'er the night!
The houses rock, in this mad weather,
While night's dark rulers come together!
Ah! oft I've seen such hideous storms,
When we have tried our secret charms!
But when weird rites we met to pay,
We met such storms without dismay.
Dread, fearful signs, I've seen and heard—
Sure, fatal, signs, that all have feared:
    At night, I've heard the cock at twelve,
Thrice warn the sexton he must delve—
That ere the morrow's clock struck one,
One more would from the earth be gone—
That death must still pursue his trade,

And one more in the earth be laid.

    I've heard the death-watch, on the wall,
Tick out his midnight, deadly call,
While listeners shook with shivering fear,
Feeling cold, grisly death was near:
New graves, they felt, must soon be made,
And death once more must prove his trade.

    At midnight, oft, I've heard the sounds
Of Gabriel hunting with his hounds;
Their fearful gabbling in the air,
Bade some doomed wretch for death prepare—
Some doomed one, perhaps not yet afraid
He in the earth must soon be laid.

    I've seen, too, at the depth of night,
Pale, ghastly, things appear in white,
Showing by looks, some withering heart
Then quivered on Death's relentless dart:
Though voiceless, still they clearly said
A corpse must in the earth be laid.

    One night the wind moaned in the clouds;
The restless dead walked in their shrouds;
The watch dog howled, the raven cried;
The while a blood-stained murderer died:
Death robbed the murderer of his trade:
The murderer in the earth is laid.

    But ere this fearful night be done,
Come, each tell how she's lost and won,

And tell what charm she's used to prove
How she must prosper in her love.

You, Elspath, first your case relate;
Say how you've tried to learn from Fate
If you, from love, will gain your due,
And if fate's promise still seems true.

ELSPATH.

When Friday night met Saturday morn,
Sowing as sowers sow their corn,
I hempseed o'er my shoulder threw,
And softly called a name I knew;
Then, as the hempseed I should sow,
I bade him bring his scythe, and mow;
And, if he e'er would be my own,
I begged his image might be shown.
But ere the words I could repeat,
His scythe was glistening at my feet;
The form I called now met my view;
But from it, I in terror flew.

MOTHER.

That night you led his ghost a dance,
And laid his body in a trance:
He felt a stupor o'er him creep,
Then sunk into a deathlike sleep,
His friends around all dumb with fear:
That moment did his ghost appear,
To show that through his future life,

You must most surely be his wife.

'Twas well you fled from him in fright,
Or you had proved, too sure, that night,
That, fast as you your hemp might sow,
He faster still, your hemp could mow.

But come now, Meg, your story tell:
Is still your lover wooing well?
Have you your lover forced to pray
That you will name the blissful day?
Or is he still the roving blade,
Not sparing either wife or maid?
How does he woo? come let us hear
If you've yet bought your wedding gear.

MEG.

The charm I use, my love to serve,
Requires, you'll say, unshrinking nerve.
But then, in love, all means are good,
E'en though they bear some stains of blood.
If we cold lovers hearts would gain,
We must not shrink from giving pain.
Nor must we fear some trifling sin,
When lover's hands we strive to win.
If blood I need, to mix my charm,
I look on blood without alarm:
But not my lover is't that bleeds;
'Tis toads blood that my mixture needs;
Which, dropt into my lover's drink,

Gives me the power, when e'er I think
His heart from me inclined to rove,
To bring him back and own his love.
Then, while the toad I still confine,
I know his heart must still be mine.
But when his love, I've cause to doubt,
I gently turn the toad about;
And be it day, or be it night,
And be it dark, or be it light,
And though he then be far away,
He rushes home without delay;
And through the fields and through the wood,
And through the bog, and through the flood,
And through the brake, and through the brier,
He comes all mad with fierce desire;
And nothing stops him, till he stands
Begging for mercy at my hands.
Thus I a truant lover rule;
I thus a truant lover cool.

MOTHER.

Ah! well I know your charm is strong;
I proved it oft when I was young:
Its power, I then had oft to try,
When he I wed grew cold and shy;
When from my toils he tried to break,
And in some rival's arms would seek
To taste the sweets of love's delight,

And rob me of my dearest right:
With it I made the wanderer feel,
From me, no foe, his heart could steal;
And though for change, his heart would burn,
He ever humbler would return:
I plagued him so with love and spite,
That he became obedient quite:
Through peace and strife, his heart I led,
Till he, at last, was fain to wed.

    But come, now, Christy, must we know
How love with you is like to go?

CHRISTY.

    Well, if I must, I must relate
How I compell my sulky fate
To show my future good or ill—
If I in love may have my will.
I'm still unwed, and wish to know
If I to church am soon to go;
And if I am, I wish to see   ·
Who must my life companion be.
Now, if my fate obeys me well,
If you will list, I now will tell:

    At midnight, when the world's asleep,
I softly from my chamber creep,
And, while the winds the sleepers rock,
In haste, I wash and wring my smock;
Before the fire with fluttering heart,

I hang it quick, and then depart.
But though my limbs may shake with fear,
I hide where I can see and here,
And mutter low, my ghostly charm,
To bring to view, some ghostly form,
Which ere my smock begins to burn,
With ghostly hands, my smock may turn;
And ere he does my presence leave,
I ask I may, his face perceive,
That I may know, when next we meet,
I then my future husband greet.
But scarce I could my words recite
Before a spectre met my sight,
And turned my smock before the fire;
Then further granted my desire,
By turning on my shuddering view,
A leering face, my heart ne'er knew—
He told me by his flashing eye,
My heart must at his mercy lie;
And as I'd seek my mate for life,
He'd seek me for his future wife.
The form then faded from my sight,
And in a swoon, I sank with fright:
I know not yet how long I lay,
But when I woke 'twas breaking day.

MOTHER.

I wonder not you swooned with fear
With such a ghostly stranger near:

You sought a form your fancy knew,
When one you knew not, met your view.
But to your fate, you must submit;
What must be, must be made to fit.

'Tis your turn, Elphie, now to tell
What heart you've brought beneath your spell,
And if you've asked your fate to show
What all our sex desire to know.

But by your smile, I see you've tried
To learn when you must be a bride,
And who he is, and what he has,
That through the church, with you must pass;
And whether he be rich or poor;
Not if a true man or a boor:
Such questions, we but seldom ask;
To promise wealth, is fortune's task.

ELPHIE.

'Tis true, I called on fate to say
What for me in the future lay:
No woman's heart, my heart would be,
Had bridal hopes no charm for me;
And as years grow, my yearnings grow,
To see what future years will show—
If he that claims me for his wife,
With wealth will bless my wedded life.
And fate has shown me in his glass,
What must, in future, come to pass;

He in his glass has let me see
The man that must my husband be.
I saw him near the alter stand,
The ring to wed me in his hand,
And I, poor fool, stood trembling near—
Trembling with joy, death-pale with fear.
I saw, too, what 'twas bliss to see,
Three darling daughters cling to me;
And what made still, my bliss more sweet,
My eager eyes, a son did greet:
Sweet light, a moment round them lay;
Then darkness swept them all away.
One daughter faded, then another;
Then with the third, death seized their brother.
I wept to see this must be so—
That such sweet joys so soon must go.
They were but as dream-pictures shown;
Yet still I loved them as my own;
And though 'twas foolish, perhaps, to weep,
That night I wept myself to sleep.
I saw my future lot in life;
I saw I soon must be a wife,
And soon a mother's joy must know,
Then feel a mother's greatest woe.
I thought no more of sordid gold—
Of wedded love e'er growing cold,
But wept that I so soon must lose
The dearest joy the mother knows.

I prayed I might the future view,
I prayed my answers might be true;
But now, the lot my fate has shown,
I pray may on me ne'er be thrown.

MOTHER.

The lot decreed you at your birth,
Would find you hid within the earth.
'Tis useless, then, your fate to grieve;
'Tis useless, now, to disbelieve,
And do as most incline to do—
Believe the good, alone, is true.
You say you in the glass descried
That soon you were to be a bride—
That soon you must a mother be—
Two joys, your heart rejoiced to see:
A wife you must be, then a mother;
Your three sweet girls must have a brother—
Three darling daughters, then a boy
Must crown your wedded life with joy.
Content, I trow, your heart had been,
Had that been all your eye had seen.
But after joy there comes a sorrow;
'Tis fair to-day, then foul to-morrow.
But still let joy possess its day;
Though sorrows come, they will not stay.
Your promised joys, you must forego,
If past your joy, you look for woe.

Think of the husband you must wed—
What must spring from your marriage bed;
For though your children may not tarry,
You'll keep the husband you shall marry.
Fate we should meet without distrust;
All fates, alike, end in the dust.

To you, sweet Prue, we turn at last,
To hear if fate, your lot has cast—
If in the day or in the night,
What future hides, has come to light—
What charm or spell, you most esteem.
Have you by sign, or morning dream,
Learnt what you must in future find?
Does what you're told content your mind?

PRUE.

I've tried to learn, by various ways,
My weal or woe of future days.
I've often prayed, while in my bed,
For dreams of him I am to wed ;
And oft when day has sunk in night,
And some new moon has met my sight,
O'er stile or gate, I've softly prayed
That in my sleep, she'd give me aid—
That if she'd power, she'd let me see
If I a wife was soon to be,
And let me know, while wrapped in sleep,
If he I loved, his faith would keep.

Then counting pins, too, from a row,
While muttering Pater Nosters low,
I've prayed before I've gone to rest,
That in my dreams I might be blest
With visions of that blissful life
That must await the new made wife:
I've prayed on sweet St. Agnes Eve
That in my dreams I might receive
My future husband's soft caresses, .
And taste the bliss the bride possesses—
Those joys that must remain untried,
Till I, myself, am made a bride.
I've prayed the fays would o'er me fling
Some spell that in my sleep would bring
My future woe and future bliss—
What must be well, and what a miss.
But spells and charms are vain 'twould seem,
For nought I see, though oft I dream.
Whatever future o'er me hovers,
Fate nought reveals of future lovers.
I dream of swelling clouds and mountains;
Of muddy streams, and crystal fountains;
Of churches, temples, new and old;
Of summer's heat, and winter's cold;
Of joys and sorrows, long since fled;
Of absent friends, acquaintance dead;
Of mourning hearts in merry meeting;
Of spiteful foes in friendly greeting;

Of silent birds, unseasoned flowers ;
Of snakes concealed in blissful bowers ;
Of singing swans, on river sailing ;
Of happy brides, their fate bewailing ;
I see the dead, dead, and still living—
The spendthrift saving, miser giving :
I dream of all things, in a jumble,
Except of him my heart would humble.
What is not, in my dreams I see ;
But not what is, or is to be.
But now, no more to dreams I look ;
My prophet now's the sacred book—
The Bible, with a key inside,
And round it, then, my garter tied ;
The key placed where sweet Ruth avows
She'll go where e'er her lover goes,
Some friend and I then hold the ring
While I to mind, my lover bring ;
And as the book a moment lingers,
While hanging on our pointed fingers,
Ruth's speech I softly then repeat,
Though with alarm, my heart should beat ;
And if I am to win my love,
The bible soon begins to move ;
And if it off my finger turn,
I learn the fate I wish to learn.
We tried this on a winter night ;
But when it turned we fled with fright :

I scarce got through the speech of Ruth
Before we learned the fearful truth,
That spirits hovering in the air,
Unseen, had heard my muttering prayer:
An answer came, from good or evil:
We fled, as if 'twere from the devil.

MOTHER.

Whether good or ill, they've power to show
What all our sex desire to know.
But when you've lived as long as I,
You'll need no more, your fortune try:
Love, that now works so sure a charm,
Will work you, then, no good or harm:
That life that yet you have to meet,
You'll find a mixture, sour and sweet;
But now, like all, you wish to see
How large a part the sweet must be?
That you must learn in growing older,
While head and heart are growing colder:
You know not, in your youthful fire,
The worth of all you now desire.
But still 'tis wise, while youth may last,
To taste youth's joys ere youth is past:
Cold age, no warmth, from youth would borrow,
If youth quenched all its heat in sorrow.
Be glad, then, while your hearts are young;
Sad youth makes short life seeming long;

And lightly trust, from day to day,
Those secrets, fate will not betray,
Are better as they are, concealed,
Till in your lives they are revealed:
Did we know all we wish to learn,
The course of fate we'd strive to turn,
And miss those checks that cool the blood,
And seeming ill, make certain good.

OLD TIME.

In Summer days, and blossomed youth,
    Old Time's a pleasant fellow;
Then fruit and wifelings have their growth
    Ere Autumn makes them mellow.
Then hungering girls and wanton boys
    Bid halting Time come faster;
He in his poke brings nuptial joys,
    And each would be a taster.
With lingering pace, Time brings the boon
    That each has been expecting;
Then nimbly skips the honey-moon,
    And leaves his friends reflecting.
His stealthy step, from stage to stage,
    Is now but seldom noted,
Till, green youth turned to withering age,
    'Tis seen how he's devoted:
Then stop, cries age, thy quickening speed,
    Or let thy pace be slower;
This once O help me in my need;
    Too soon I meet the mower.

LUCY, THE DESERTED.

Slowly are the shadows stealing
   Up the breast of yonder hill;
Still is gentle Lucy kneeling;
   Wearily she's kneeling still.

Silently the dews are falling
   In the steps of fleeing day;
Still is Lucy faintly calling
   On a name now far away.

On the hill the day is dying;
   Shadows o'er the valley hover;
Deeply still is Lucy sighing—
   Sighing for a faithless lover.

In the west, the day is sleeping;
   O'er us, night has thrown his veil;
Still with sobs, is Lucy weeping—
   Weeping still with tearless wail.

When the morning comes to-morrow,
   Making all hearts once more glad,
Lucy still will be in sorrow;
   Evermore she will be sad.

Who could wound a heart so tender?
   Who could blight so sweet a form?
Who would pray not heaven may send her
   Vengeance for her cruel harm?

Who can see her killing trouble
   Eat away a life so sweet,
And not wish her wronger double
   Those fierce woes th' accursed meet?

Sadly must we now remember
   How she sung her hours away—
How she left her peaceful slumber
   When the lark awoke the day.

When the thrush, high mounted, singing,
   Lulled the day to sweet repose,
Then her voice would, softly ringing,
   Bless the summer evening's close.

All who knew her, knew her gladly;
   All who saw her, sought her smile;
All hence forth must know her sadly—
   Victim sad of fiendish guile.

Speechless be their tongues forever,
   Who such trusting ones deceive;
May they truth believe in never;
   May they lies alone believe.

Be their hearts with torture riven;
   May they know hell's pain and live;
May no help to them be given,
   Till they curse the woes they give.

THE REJECTED LOVER.

The wan moon has now set,
And I'm still wandering yet,
As I've wandered, alone, through the night ;
I still feel her hard scorn,
While this beautiful morn
Fills, again, the sad heavens with his light.

To my plea, she said no ;
And she then bade me go—
Go and leave her, she'd see me no more ;
I then spoke not a word ;
I no more then implored ;
But such anguish, I ne'er felt before.

O how bitter her scorn,
On this beautiful morn!
Sweet peace will return to me never !
How different now this light
Had appeared to my sight,
Had she said she would love me forever.

O why should my fate be
That so she should hate me,
And make me so poor and forlorn ?

Had she owned that she loved,
My glad heart, now had proved
The full bliss of this beautiful morn.

She knows how I love her;
But that will not move her;
She turned from my tears with a frown;
While she still heard me pray,
She turned coldly away:
If she felt, she no feeling would own.

In the world, I'm obscure;
And in gold, too, I'm poor;
With my gold, I can ne'er buy her heart;
If for station and gold,
She her sweet self has sold,
'Tis hard, though 'tis best that we part.

Still, with gold I should try her,
If with gold I could by her,
Though 'twould grieve me to know she was bought;
But to me she's so dear,
That should hope but come near,
Her heart would seem pure as my thought.

But I ne'er now must see
Her sweet smile rest on me;
Her dark frown, now, must haunt me forever;
My hot words winged with love,
Her cold heart ne'er could move:
Now all hope, from my heart I must sever.

Through dark woods I may wander,
Or where sad streams meander,
And watch the glad bird woo its mate;
But my sad heart, alone,
Or with sad hearts that moan,
May bewail the hard dealings of fate.

When sad night's again set
With its rich golden fret,
And the heavens have extinguished their flame,
I again, forth may wander,
On my sad fate to ponder;
But pondering and wandering leave my heart still
the same.

Night and day now are one;
Life's sweet hope now is gone;
All my life's joy in hope is now blighted;
Through each night till the morn,
I must still nurse her scorn—
The cold scorn which my warm love so slighted.

But I'm still wandering yet,
Though the cold moon has set,
With no feeling of ought but her scorn;
Though my tears ne'er could move her,
My heart still must love her:
O how hard is my fate to be born!

MY FOUR-FOOTED FRIEND.

We hear vows of friendship,
　　And some vows seem sincere ;
Men oft deeply swear,
　　To their vows they'll adhere ;
But though men deeply swear
　　They'll be true to the end,
They're ne'er half so true as
　　My four-footed friend.

In seeking for friendship,
　　Man sometimes seeks pleasure ;
Though often he seeks but
　　For fortune and treasure ;
But true unbought friendship,
　　Who would e'er comprehend,
Must study the heart of
　　My four-footed friend.

The treasure he seeks is
　　Wrapped up in his dinner ;
His fortune, he finds in
　　The smiles of a sinner;
Though kindness delight him,
　　Yet frowns went offended :
Through all moods there's faith in
　　My four-footed friend.

In bright days of summer,
    When light gentle breeze
Makes soft whispering music
    Among the green trees,
In my long rural rambles,
    No one else will attend,
I've a faithful companion in
    My four-footed friend.

Though words are denied him,
    I still know his mind;
In his large speaking eye,
    His true meaning I find;
From the shake of his tail,
    I his wish comprehend:
My friend is not dumb, though
    A four-footed friend.

Let me, then, kindly treat
    The affectionate creature,
And meet with good faith,
    The good faith of his nature;
If from hunger and harm,
    I poor Jack wont defend,
Where may kindness be found by
    My four-footed friend.

DEATH OF MY FOUR-FOOTED FRIEND.

Farewell! dear companion;
  Death now bids us part;
He rends the dear ties
  Thou hast wound round my heart:
I dreamt not thy life
  Drew so near to its end,
Or I still more had loved thee,
  My four-footed friend.

Now in bright days of summer,
  The soft whispering breeze
Makes no more cheerful music
  Among the green trees:
In my lone rural rambles,
  Thou no more must attend,
I shall heave many a sigh for
  My four-footed friend.

I shall miss thy large eyes,
  Which oft dwelt on my face,
When I plucked some fresh flower,
  Or some new thought would trace,
And the hint thou wouldst gambol,
  When 'twas time I should spend
A word or a look on
  My four-footed friend.

When, alone, I shall ramble,
  In the fine summer weather,
Through the scenes where so oft
  We've been lonely together,
I shall pause in my thought,
  When the mind would unbend,
And look through a tear for
  My four-footed friend.

All those dearly loved spots,
  We both hied to with gladness,
Are now left alone in
  The cold shade of sadness;
Joy's thrill, through the heart,
  They no more now can send;
They chill now with grief for
  My four-footed friend.

I loved thee—thou knew'st it,
  And my love did'st return;
When it seemed lost in coldness,
  Thou its loss then would'st mourn;
But coldness, or harshness,
  Thy true faith ne'er could bend:
None can e'er fill thy place,
  My four-footed friend.

AIR:—FLOATING ON THE WIND.

Smiling ever near,
　Unseen friends abide,
Warding doubt and fear,
　Ever from my side—
Smiling on the heart ;
　Breathing holy thoughts—
Thoughts that love impart—
　Love that never doubts :
Love wings the soul away
　To joys bright summer day—

Smiling ever near—
　Whispering to the heart
Change it need not fear,
　Joy will ne'er depart—
Hope's bright radiant light,
　Beaming through the soul—
Love forever bright,
　Time can ne'er controll :
Joy ne'er shall know decay,
　Through love's bright summer day.

AN UNSPOKEN ADDRESS.

I come, good friends, obedient to your call;
And most sincerely, would I thank you all,
Not for the kindness of to-night, alone,
But that, as well you in the past have shown.
I well remember—can I e'er forget,
While still unpaid, is nature's final debt?
I still remember well, that trembling day,
When with your heartfelt cheer, I went away—
When, winged with hope, young aspiration flew
To scenes untried, and bade old friends adieu.
My course, since then, through light and shade has
          lain;
But with glad heart, I've met you here again;
And still your kindness greets me as of yore:
Still once more I must leave you, as before.
    When duty calls, her call we must obey;
For duty rules even our poor actor's day;
Though some deem, perhaps, we know not duty's
          rule;
But such deem not the theatre a school—
A school where human nature we may see,
Oft as it is, oft as it ought to be

We see rash youth, blind passion's wasteful slave—
Weak fretful age stand chaffering near the grave:
When passions burn, hot youth counts not the cost;
Cold age seeks most to save, when all is lost.
As nature's page, keen-eyed experience reads,
The fool of age, the fool of youth succeeds.
Both fools and knaves we see, and both dispise;
We see, and loath, the man of pious lies.
We see the scoundrel, whom at once we hate,
And gladly watch the villian seek his fate.
But these are failures, dropt from nature's plan;
In nature's noblest work, we see the man.
Not him whose choice at nature's bounteous feast,
Is that which makes the man subserve the beast;
Nor that void thing made by convention's law,
And ruled then by some solemn, selfish, saw;
Who brags perfection in each human part,
Though destitute where should be head and heart;
But him 'twas nature's highest aim to make,
Content to work long ages for his sake;
Whose life, from head and heart, is always one—
Brave, generous, just, and truthful as the sun;
Who scans the heavens, with eye and mien erect,
Melts worlds to light, to feed his intellect;
Whose heart and eye oft glow with passions' fire,
Yet still ne'er severs duty from desire:
We with delight, see such upon the stage;
With fruitful love, such must our hearts engage.

Thus docile pupils learn at Thespia's school
To love the man, and scorn the knave and fool.
   Some words, to these, I fear I might annex,
That slightly touch some frailties of my sex;
But these, the censors of our sex will name:
We may not praise ourselves, and will not blame;
Not that we'er dumb, no, not by any means;
Our tongues can trot, when once they take the reins;
But that's not oft, as you must all allow:
But waiving that, my tongue is silent now.
The main of what I've said, you know is true;
Believe this, too, my heart now says adieu.

AN EPILOGUE.

M.

You see, good friends, our play is done;
And if we've your approval won,
We've gained the end we all intended:
If not, we wish the thing were mended.
The matter's old; but that you know—
As old as human weal and woe;
Yet though 'tis old, it is not trite;
'Tis ever fresh as day and night.
Ere plays were played, or words were writ,
It charmed the tongue of human wit;
And ere it cease, man's heart to move—
Ere man turn cold from woman's love,
The sun shall fly through boundless space;
Each little star shall lose its place;
And night no longer twain with day,
Shall hold o'er all, eternal sway.

L.

If with our play you're interested,
You'll perhaps allow that I'm invested
With right, before you go away,
To tell what woman's slanderers say

They say our love is merely trade,
By which our social rank is made;
That though with men we gladly yoke,
Our flame, they say, is only smoke.
'Twere pity such should find us true:
To such, is true love ever due?
You'll answer that as well as I:
To those, then, let us say good bye.
But let our hearts once know their own,
Then judge us by the love that's shown;
Let native worth, our hearts subdue,
Then ask us if our hearts are true.

B.

If I might here but make so bold,
I'd say, man's love's not always cold;
Some times it feels as hot as bricks:
But then, the girls, they play such tricks!
There's Jenny, here, the other day,
She boxed my ear, then ran away.
I doubt she wanted me to follow,
And catch her in the primrose hollow,
And there, for all her jibes and teezing,
She thought she'd get an honest squeezing.
If she were pleased with what befel,
I leave her pouting lips to tell.

But now we leave this playful strife;
She's promised soon to be my wife:
Of wedded life he speaks to soon,
Who speaks before the honeymoon.

J.

You've heard his way of speaking boldly;
You've heard him boast of wooing coldly:
I thought his manner quite provoking;
I ne'er could tell if he were joking.
He said he loved; I wished to know it;
I boxed his ear, to make him show it:
Now my poor lips, he dares to say
How rude he was in that affray;
As if he'd done some great exploit:
They view it in a different light.
How much so e'er they felt their wrong,
They're able still to hold their tongue.
'Tis prudence, not to speak too soon:
We've not yet reached the honeymoon.
His moon of sweets will pass no doubt;
He'll then, perhaps, hear my tongue speak out.

F.

I'll just say, ere the curtain fall,
Good night, my friends, God bless you all.

EPITAPHS.

I.

A friend here sleeps, alas! beneath this stone!
  A friend whom time, to me will not restore!
Her silent heart but now is truly known
  To him who mourns its silence ever more.
No self-regard could move her constant mind;
  No voice but tender duty's could she hear;
In other's good, life's joy her heart could find;
  No peace she knew, with wrong and misery near:
One word sums up the the virtues of her life,
One tearful word: She was, indeed, my wife!

II.

This mortal me, that served my mortal hour,
Now melts to clay beneath death's mortal power;
The sins it sinned, I pray pass unregarded;
What worth it had, with worth was well rewarded.

III.

Our rose bud bloomed an hour, then passed away;
  Death-nipt, it blooms for us on earth no more;
Yet in hope's realm it blooms in nightless day,
  And blooms in sweeter beauty than before.

A SONNET.

She's dead! O God how lonely am I now!
    What now on earth may cheer this dreary life!
No rest, again on earth, my heart can know,
    But with fierce grief must wage unending strife.
Alone I wander through the silent woods,
    Where oft, rejoicing, she has been with me!
I stand alone! my tears burst forth in floods!
    My streaming eyes, nowhere her form can see.
At night, heart-weary night! I home return—
    The home she made, but now no longer home!—
Now but a place where sleepless nights I mourn,
    Or pray, with morn, an endless night may come.
But night nor day can bring again repose,
Till pitying death my term of suff'ring close.

FLORENCE.

Hymn and Tune for a Friend.

O, blest im - mor - tal an - gels, come, And

aid my soul to rise; Make sure my heart, ex-alt my mind, My

hopes turn to the skies, My hopes turn to the skies.

2. While still sojourning here below,
   Keep me from sin and fear ;
   Whene'er temptation cross my path,
   Some saving help be near.

3. The righteous law, by Heaven ordained,
   Incline me to obey :
   My faltering step, make firm and sure ;
   Let wisdom light my way.

4. With grateful love my heart endue,
   To God for blessings given ;
   More worthy make me, still to see
   The loving smile of Heaven.

5. When death's dark shadows round me grow,
   And mortal toil must cease,
   May I, with joy, the hour approach,
   In hopes of blissful peace.

SERENADE.

From an unpublished Play.

Lo! in the east the day is born, And gladness swells each tune-ful voice; Flow'rs breathe sweet welcome to the morn, And Na-ture bids all hearts re-joice. O come, O Come, come Na-ture's fairest an-gel, come; O come, O come, O come, O come, O come, give new de-light to Nature's home, O come, give new de-light to Nature's home.

2. The daisy, gemmed wi' pearls o' dew,
  Has smiled farewell to parting night;
The lark soars in the heavenly blue,
  To greet the morning with delight.
O come, come Nature's fairest angel, come;
O come, give new delight to Nature's home.

3. The unseen guardians of her sleep,
  That fancy feed with rosy dreams,
Have gone their matin hour to keep,
  And bathe in morning's radiant beams.
O come, come Nature's fairest angel, come;
O come, give new delight to Nature's home.

JOHNTY AND DINAH,

BY

PHINEAS PHILGRO.

INTRODUCTION.

LETTERS FROM AND TO THE AUTHOR.

MY DEAR GREAVES:

I write to beg a favor ; or rather, I write to beg you will allow me to confer a favor upon you ; for, to speak with a friend's candour, I must tell you plainly that you ought, though I dare say you will not, consider it a great privilege to aid, in any measure, the important work I am engaged upon. But let that matter adjust itself as it may : I will come to the point at once.

You know, of course, how deeply concerned I am for the welfare of humanity; and how terribly I feel my share of responsibility for for its well-being in the future—for the well-being, most especially, of that branch of it to which I have the misfortune to belong. You know how sad and hopeless are my forebodings with regard to the destiny of this great American family, unless some check be applied to its manifest degeneracy, and, I fear, ultimate decay. Consider the momentous question calmly, my dear friend ; and if you cannot adopt my views (alas ! it is not every one that can see a manifest truth)—I say if you cannot adopt my views, I am sure you will— you must sympathise with me in my sorrow and anxiety. Let me state the case: There are here, upon this continent, some thirty or forty million individuals of our own particular branch of the human family, brought here by hard necessity from a distant quarter of the old world; and as you are well aware, every year adds to their numbers; and, alas! every year adds some new sign of their degeneracy— I say there are here these thirty or forty millions of white, or rather pale-very pale, emaciated people upon this continent, shivering down their rapid descent to their inevitable doom; while there are, mingling amongst them, some four million dusky individuals of a younger, and more vigorous branch of our species, brought here for

(185)

our salvation, as I think, by a farseeing Providence, from another distant quarter of the old world. Ah! could the rich, luscious blood of these four million be poured into the veins, and mingled with the corrupt and impoverished blood of the unfortunate forty millions!—But I will not repeat myself: I have already shown the world—at least the small portion of it that would listen to me—I say I have, already, shown the world what blessed fruit might spring from mingling the blood of the two races!

Here, then, is my request: You contemplate publishing. I, too would again stand forth before the world; but my poor, desiccated brain (due entirely to the unmixed condition of my blood,) can afford me nothing but a few feeble lines—too few and feeble to stand alone; I am, therefore, reduced to the necessity of begging you will let my poor trifle have a small space besides your own more ample thoughts when you send them forth to take the air. I do not forget that we differ as day and night on the question of mixing the races; but then, I, also, do not forget that you possess that broad catholicity of sentiment, which, with fairplay, fears neither lies, nor the father of lies. Should you refuse me, however, I shall fear I am mistaken as to the liberality of your spirit; and I shall tell you, frankly, that I think you are afraid—that I suspect you do not feel quite certain of your ability to prove that white is not the whiter for the addition of a little black.

Confidently awaiting your reply

I am, now as ever,

Willing to oblige or be obliged,

Your true friend,

PHINEAS PHILGRO.

———

My Dear Philgro,

From the many hints you have let fall in our late disputes, I anticipated some thing of your present very agreable request. I felt quite certain you would, in some way, endeavour to confer upon me the inestimable "privilege" of becoming a partner in your "momentous philantropic duties." I felt quite certain of this; but I felt quite as certain I should decline the honour; yea, though we should become eternal strangers in consequence. What the—But I will not use strong language. I will be calm. But what I say, have I to do with the different races of mankind? Did I place them upon the earth? and now that they are here, am I accountable for their weakness and imperfection? Am I charged with the duty of opposing fate, and with making any, or all of them a fixture upon the earth? Am I to consider myself a criminal if I do not try to turn the course of that particular race, which, as you say, is rushing down its rapid descent to its inevitable doom? Preach till you are speechless, my friend, if you will; but you preach to the deaf. We pitiable and, much-bepitied individuals of the doomed race, have a strong fancy for following the bent of our own sweet inclination and instincts, regardless of consequences; and I can assure you, my friend, it will require a louder and sweeter voice then yours, to persuade us to forego our present pleasures, in order to procure some very questionable advantage for some, perhaps, very questionable people in the far off future. No, no, my dear mourner; we are attending to our own immediate affairs. We are too busy endeavouring to provide for the many present, urgent wants of our own, to concern ourselves about the troubles of those that may follow us. But this doomed and decaying race, which you are so much concerned about, and to which you have the misfortune to belong? Has it not already existed for thousands, some say hundreds of thousands of years,—nay some say even for millions of years it has existed upon the earth; and would it have become totally extinct if you had not appeared, to teach it how its existence may be perpetuated? It will last my time at all events; and if it cannot keep its nose above the clover when I am gone, that is not my affair. I say again, I am not the author of my race; nor shall I consider myself responsible for its weakness and imperfections.

But have you, indeed, the presumption to suppose, (I speak with a friend's candor),—I say, have you the presumption to suppose the continuance of your race depends on any thing that may flow from your "poor desiccated brain;"—that if it will not recuperate itself according to your delectable theory, it must melt from the face of the earth like snow in a great thaw? and that this continent will again become a wilderness, again given up to the red man and the buffalo? Once more I say it will last my time; and for the rest, what is that to me? Nay, I firmly believe it will continue 'till it has used up its limited stock of coal and timber; and when it is compelled to seek some new method of bottling the summer's sunshine to keep itself from freezing in the winter, perhaps it might not matter much if the red man should resume possession for an age or two. But your request—the favour you would confer upon me? I have vowed—almost sworn—I would have nothing whatever to do with your rubbish—I mean your lines. But you know my weakness, you cunning man. You talk of my catholicity of sentiment—of my readiness, at all times, to pit truth against a lie, without fear of the result. You know I never could stand that kind of

flattery. You have conquered. Your-what-do-you-call-it shall
have an airing, the consequence be what it may. But I make this
stipulation, and under no circumstances will I budge from it. I
stipulate, formally and solemnly, that my share in this business
shall not bind me to carry your principles into effect. In whatever
contracts I may, in future, find it expedient to form with the other
sex, I shall firmly assert my full right and liberty to choose according to my own inclination. Though I may assist in giving your
abominable doctrine to the world, I solemnly protest that I will not
reduce it to practice in my own person. A few shades one might
not object to, perhaps, but a full dip! I will not think of it. With
this condition fairly understood, I submit to your favour and con-
sent to be—

Your much obliged friend,

A. GREAVES.

My Dear Greaves:

You have consented to give my "abominable doctrine" an "airing." I knew you would. Call it what you please, so that you
give it a fair chance. You protest you will not reduce my "abominable doctrine" to practice? But you solemnly protested, you
know, you would have nothing to do with its publication. One
thing at a time. I know you my friend. One thing at a time I say.
I have hopes. I enclose you the "rubbish" with this. Look it
over and let me know what you think of it. But, of course, I
know what you will say. I am, as before,

Your obliged and obliging friend,

PHINEAS PHILGRO.

My Dear Philgro,

I have read your—I will not give it a name—I am committed.
Had the stuff been ten times more distasteful, I am pledged to pub-
lish it. But can you say, with any pretention to conscience, that
you have not taken an unfair and dishonorable advantage of me?
Have you not most outragiously abused the condfience I placed in
you? However, I am committed; and I cannot retreat. If you are
not ashamed to tell the world you are ready to put away your own
lawfully wedded wife, and take ten others in her place, the very
least I can say, (for I am determined to be moderate,) you ought
to be ashamed to set yourself up as a teacher of anything. Still
I must keep my word, My only hope is, the world will see how
very reluctantly I have come into this very disagreable business

Yours, much mortified,

A. GREAVES.

JOHNTY AND DINAH.

How! O how I worship thee,
Goddess of my destiny!
O how thy dusky tyranny
Has bound my heart in slavery!

Break, O break, my galling chain!
Quench, O quench my burning pain!
Let me taste sweet peace again,
And ever in thy heart remain.

Ease, O ease my bitter smart!
Let me still be where thou art!
Bid me not from thee depart;
Or break, O break my doomed heart!

———

Some days ago, no matter where,
In strolling forth to take the air,
As carelessly I on was walking,
I chanced to hear a couple talking:
I heeded not their conversation,
'Till I heard 'twas on miscegenation.
Bless me, thought I, but that 's a subject,
To hear discussed, I must not neglect:

(189)

Especially as here the sexes
Are as nature needs them when she mixes.
It may not, perhaps, be thought polite
To listen first, and then to write
What boys and girls say when they woo—
How foolishly they bill and coo;
But this, I think, my case excuses:
My tale has philantrophic uses,
And must be heard in public places,
By all who wish to mix the races.

But let's no more our tale preface,
But let the woosters take their place;
And Dinah's voice, we'll first give ear to;
But slight her, let us not appear to;
For though she's black, she's worth attention,
As you'll perceive by what I mention.

Johnty, (her lover's name was Johnty,
The woe-worn nephew of his Aunty),
Good Gracious, Johnty, don't you flatter?
You used to curse me like a hatter,
And call me names, for instance skunk;
You seemed to think a body stunk;
You would not work with me, nor pray,
Nor ride with me, at least by day;
You would not join me in my creed;
And now you'd join with me to breed.
But goodness Johnty, this is strange;
Who'd e'er have thought of such a change?
But let me see; miscegenation?
That's mixing for a generation?

I own the matter's quite provoking :
But then, dear Johnty, aint you joking ?
   Joking, dear Dinah, did you say ?
I never joke : 'tis not way :
I ne'er indulge in sinful nonsense :
Joking agrees not with my conscience.
I think of nothing but my duty,
Except my Dinah's precious beauty—
A beauty so fat, rich and luscious !
Which makes me feel this moment just as
If I'd drunk divine elixer—
Some regular youth-and-beauty fixer :
Nay e'en the smell of her sweet body
Revives me like the fumes o' toddy.
   O golly, Johnty, this is bully ;
But don't you see my head is woolly ?
And that I'm black as Aunty's stove ?
But nothing is so blind as love.
   Your doubts, dear Dinah, how they shock me !
I hope you don't intend to mock me ?
Or think, with you I fear to pair,
Because you're black with woolly hair ?
These are but signs that you're the creature,
From sunny south, designed by nature
To renovate my shriveling form
With tropic juice, thick, rich and warm,
And save me from my pending doom,
And bear me past a threatening tomb.
   O, Johnty dear, you are so pressing,
I can't refuse some slight caressing.

But then, dear Johnty, how 'll we do it?
If you should wed, you perhaps might rue it;
The other way, we've often tried it;
But preachers say we should avoid it.
To either way, I've no objection;
Yet sin, you know, meets such correction
That, though I own my blood is warm,
I must say nay, if but for form.
  O Dinah, dear, my jetty jewel,
Pray hear me speak, and don't be cruel:
My piteous case, I lay before you;
Look on 't, dear Dinah, I implore you.
Though young in years, I'm old and battered;
My bloodless frame is worn and shattered.
My pate, too, Dinah, 's bare and cold;
The people sware I'm growing old:
What hair I have is harsh and scanty,
And turning gray before I'm twenty.
O spare me from that poll of thine
A little wool to plant on mine.
O save me from my piteous fate!
Or still more sufferings must I state?
My eyes are bleared; my teeth are rotten;
My body's lank—my belly shotten;
While you 're as plump as purple peaches,
I'm skin and bone in boots and breeches.
O Dinah, dear, pray have compassion;
Don't leave me shriveling in this fashion,
But give me from thy juicy nature
Some pulp, to fill my shrunken feature;

And do not mind the parson's racket,
But stuff my pants and pad my jacket.
But I'm exhausted with my feeling,
While trembling at your feet I'm kneeling,
Begging you 'll hear my sad confession,
And grant me sure and swift possession
Of means to save my dwindling breed—
Your own sweet self, my nature's need—
   But here I heard a hasty hustle;
I thought it might be Dinah's bustle,
'Till Johnty cried, as out he rushes :
A rival 's sneaking round the bushes !
I heard his low infernal hissing ;
It sounded just like Dinah's kissing.
My curses on him and his race !
He's crawling round in every place ;
One can't perform the meanest duty,
Not even taste of Dinah's beauty,
But he's at hand, to strike with dread,
And knock one's courage on the head.
But come, my Dinah, let's be goin',
And seek some other place to woo in.
The best of folks may make mistakes :
We'll mix it yet, in spite of snakes ;
Our blood we'll yet amalgamate,
And such a brood we'll procreate
As o'er the world shall reign supreme,
And change the whole of nature's scheme :
I then can cry to all creation,
My Dinah's brought me sweet salvation.

This tale I tell with grief profound,
For I'm in wedlock firmly bound.
And sadder still, (I speak with shame),
My partner's white, and I'm the same.
But duty's stern imperious force
Bids me at once to seek divorce—
Put off my wife, and in her place,
Take one of Dinah's luscious race.
The task is hard, but I can do it:
I can, I vow, as I'm a poet;
Nay, were there ten put in her place,
I'd take them all, to mix my race.

Now boys and girls take my advice,
And weigh it well before you splice;
Hear duty's call while still you're single,
And let white blood, with black blood mingle;
Don't mix and wed with one another;
Let each white girl choose some black brother—
Each boy look out, before he wed,
Some sable partner for his bed.
And thus we'll make that glorious mixture
Which on the earth, shall prove a fixture;
And for those ills of blood that's pure,
We'll work an everlasting cure.

THE END.

www.ingramcontent.com/pod-product-compliance
Lightning Source LLC
Chambersburg PA
CBHW030540040726
47497CB00008B/2535